T0195871

SAWDUST
AND
SPLINTERS

'There be Money in them Trees'

WORKING WITH WOOD SINCE BEFORE 1750

SHOPLAND'S CLEVEDON SAWMILLS

1860 - 2020

David W Shopland

Order this book online at www.trafford.com
or email orders@trafford.com

Most Trafford titles are also available at major online book retailers.

Print information available on the last page.

ISBN: 978-1-6987-1157-7 (sc)
ISBN: 978-1-6987-1156-0 (hc)
ISBN: 978-1-6987-1155-3 (e)

Library of Congress Control Number: 2022905376

Trafford rev. 10/06/2022

www.trafford.com
North America & international
toll-free: 844-688-6899 (USA & Canada)
fax: 812 355 4082

This book has been an exercise of my memory and regretfully I am not infallible, so if anyone has been left out, treated unfairly or some facts are wrong, the fault is entirely mine. The photographs are largely from the Family archives and again, if I have inadvertently infringed any copyright or caused any offence, I apologise unreservedly, and if it is possible, I will endeavour to put things right.

David W Shopland
August 2022

ROLL OF HONOUR

SAMUEL GENGE

HARRY SCRIBBINS

CHARLIE MARTIN

In Grateful Memory of the above who were killed
when working for the Shopland Family.

CLEVEDON

THE GEM OF SUNNY SOMERSET

THE HOME OF THE SAWMILLS

Esplanade and Victorian Pier

Clevedon is situated on the coast in the County of Somerset which is in the West of England near Bristol, where the Severn River merges into the Bristol Channel and the Atlantic. It is a place where Turner, the famous Painter, drew inspiration for his depictions of glorious sunsets, if it is a dark, clear night, you can see a light shining far out to sea in the West and it is said that the light is possibly on top of the Statue of Liberty in New York as there is nothing but sea in between, though it is more likely to be a light ship off the Welsh coast.

It is not a place where too much had happened to give it a claim to lasting fame, except maybe it was where Penicillin was discovered and developed during WW2, it was visited by some Poets (including Coleridge, Tennyson, Hallam), General W. Booth (founder of the Salvation Army), General Buller who was the General who relieved Mafeking in the Boer War, and Lloyd George (the Liberal Prime Minister of WW1).

At the beginning of the 1800s, Clevedon was a village with a population of around 300, and when William arrived by train in the 1850s, Clevedon was really still only a large village owned by several wealthy Families who mostly lived in new upper-class houses on the Hill above the Triangle and Old Street. The remainder was mostly small Farms, fields, little groups of Cottages and the Parish Church of St Andrews which was the only place of worship. There were no paved roads, only muddy tracks in winter or dust trails in summer, with the occasional covering layer of loose stones placed on the surface near a posh house which could afford it. The tracks had no drainage, though there might have been a few Pennant Kerb Stones from Conygar Quarry laid to delineate the odd pavement. Water supplies still came from private wells or the rivers and the House sewers were mostly private systems, which led to the rivers in the lower part of the town; for those living on or near to the Beach the sea gave an admirable drainage service, and hopefully, cesspits served the remainder, all of which probably made the sanitary arrangements less than satisfactory when the summer sun was shining. But it was no different from any other small aspiring seaside resorts of those times, and such happenings were acceptable, especially as in Victorian England, the sensibilities in cases of delicate 'pongs' or aromas were at times not too refined.

Later in the Century, the Railway arrived bringing Industry and Tourists, this resulted in more houses being built and Clevedon become a small seaside resort, and later a little Town with a Governing Board or Council, a Water Company, a Steam-roller, semi-paved roads, a Fire Brigade, and a new regulated Sewerage system.

Since then, many have found Clevedon to be an attractive place to live and visit, which has resulted in the number of people living here gradually rising to five thousand in 1900 and ten thousand in 1939. After which, it increased steadily until it reached today's figure of about twenty-four thousand. The Shoplands are grateful to be amongst that number and hope to remain in Clevedon for a long time to come.

<u>Golden Jubilee Triangle Clock</u>
<u>Queen Victoria's Coronation, Golden Jubilee Triangle Clock.</u>

Clevedon's Keeper of the Hours through the Years with three faces showing the Time and the North Face being an Elton Ware Mosaic portraying the 'Grim Reaper' with his Scythe, namely 'Father Time'.

The Men who created the Sawmills

William Shopland (1841–1908)

'THE FOUNDER'

Who was brave enough to leave home and travel to a new 'county' where he set the goals and laid the foundations for the future growth of his Family and their enterprises.

Edmund Henry Shopland (1872–1954)

'THE VISIONARY'

Who had the necessary enthusiasm and drive to achieve his Father's ambitions and make them secure.

Herbert Wynne Shopland (1898–1981)

'THE NEGOTIATOR AND FACILITATOR'

Who sacrificed his personal dreams and ambitions to make it all work.

David William Shopland

'THE BENEFICIARY AND FOLLOWER'

Who struggled hard and kept it all going.

James Herbert Shopland

'THE FUTURE'

Who is endeavouring to transform the company
into a new thriving concern trading as
Shoplands, The Clevedon Sawmills Ltd.

THE CLEVEDON SAWMILLS SAGA

"We cannot tell how long the road will be. We only know that it will be stony, painful, uphill and that we will march along it to the end."
Winston Spencer Churchill – May 1941.

PREFACE

This is not intended to be an exhaustive and detailed History of the Home-Grown English Timber Trade and has only been written in answer to requests to record the history of E H SHOPLAND & SON CLEVEDON SAWMILLS and create a foundation on which further research could be based, in order to gain a true picture of how Shopland's Sawmill has grown and fitted into Clevedon's ongoing development. It is a record of several determined men, at a particular moment in time, doing the best that they could in difficult and changing circumstances with few ready financial resources at hand and gives a little insight into the thinking behind their actions. Maybe with hindsight, different choices and better decisions should have been made, but they were made in good faith and in the belief that they were the best that could be done at the time.

The Shoplands, like many others in the Home-Grown Timber Trade, had been brought up in long-standing Non-conformist traditions—in their case, the Plymouth Brethren—who had deep religious principles and an unshakeable belief in a divine Providence, which, despite all trials and troubles, would somehow ensure that all was well at the end. To show their belief in a practical form, they allowed no business transaction or work to take place on a Sunday, and the Family have always tried to keep true to that tradition.

Whether or not I am the best person to write what follows is possibly open to question, but having been involved with the Sawmills for over eighty years and being one of the few left who knew it before WW2, took part in many of the events, worked with and talked to some of those who knew William and his ways possibly means that at this moment in time, I am one of the few who can write this record.

THE STORY

Family records place a John Shopland working a saw pit at Newton St Cyres in Devon during the mid 1700s, though there are stories of previous generations working with wood in Exeter. John later moved to Cullompton to marry, and it was from there that his son William moved by train to Clevedon in the 1850s with just a bag of carpenter's tool, a violin, and the clothes that he stood up in. On arriving in Clevedon, he earn't enough money to pay for his night's lodgings by playing his violin for people to dance to. Later, after settling in, he sent for his Brother John, who was living in Bridgwater, and they set up a business trading as Shopland Brothers Builders, with a view to building houses to let or sell, with a small Sawmill as an ancillary project.

After a while, the Brothers decided to dissolve their Partnership, with John doing building and William setting up a house and yard at Devonshire Place in Old Street, where he started a business which, as well as housebuilding, included carpentry, cart construction, wheelwrighting, blacksmithing, undertaking, sawmilling, and anything else that might make a shilling. Why William chose Old Street as a base is not now known, and it might have been because there was building land for sale there or that the Lord of the Manor, while not wanting Shoplands as near neighbours, decided that they had better be somewhere where he could keep his eye on them. Though as Roman coinage from around AD 150 was found near the site of the present Sawmills, so maybe Julius Caesar had a say in the matter of making it possibly the oldest trading site in the Town.

Communication with the outside world was always a problem as the business started well before the age of the telephone, and I suspect that in the early days of the Family enterprises, all the transactions and letters would have been laboriously written in longhand on plain paper and recorded the same way probably using Goose feather quills until a change to Turkey for Christmas Dinner brought steel-nibbed pens into use. Therefore, it must have been a major landmark and cause for jubilation in Family History when the first letterheads were printed and the telephone installed, for their purchase must have meant that Shoplands had made some money and could have signified to them and others that they had 'arrived' and were on the way up.

A William Shopland Letterhead

Earlier in 1866, William felt well enough established in his new premises to publish a catalogue showing what he could make and provide. Unfortunately, the cover is not in a fit state to be reproduced, but on the maroon-coloured cover, it says in gold type:

CLEVEDON STEAM WHEEL & CARRIAGE WORKS
WM. SHOPLAND
COACH BUILDER & WHEELWRIGHT
CLEVEDON

Whether William built any carriages to sell is not known now, but it is doubtful as the majority of the few wealthy people living in Clevedon had Town Houses elsewhere in the Cities where there were many excellent carriage makers, so I have only included the following examples of his craft as they would have been the type of vehicle most in demand locally.

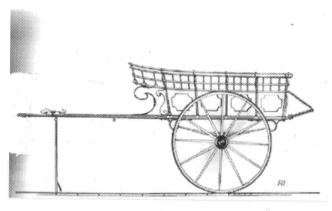

High Cart

Having a straight axle, large wheels, and a high floor, it was used for carrying small items and as a Family Cart for outings, almost the poorer man's gig. Often favoured by Gypsies and Tinkers and drawn by a cob.

Crank axle cart

Having a cranked U-shaped axle, which gave it a low level floor and enabled small goods to be easily loaded, such as small livestock, and it was also generally used by Milkmen for their deliveries when they carried several churns.

Farm Waggon

Its design was adapted and scaled down from the much-larger waggons used to travel on the primitive tracks of the Middle Ages for long-distance haulage, which had very wide-rimmed wheels and were normally drawn by a span of eight or ten oxen or sometimes a team of heavy horses. The smaller version shown above was used in the late 1800s and up to the 1940s by Farmers to haul hay or corn sheaves from the Harvest fields, grain to Mills, and root crops. Most Counties had their own individualistic designs.

Heavy Cart

Which was used by Contractors and others for transporting heavier loads of up to three tons, pulled by large, heavy horses such as Shires, Clydesdales, Suffolk Punch, etc.

Felling and cutting timber had always been hard work and had involved mainly axe work, but as things developed and improved during the seventeen hundreds, Iron or steel handsaws were being increasingly used in the Timber Trade for felling and cross-cutting trees into manageable lengths. From very early times, producing planks or beams had involved the use of wedges to split the trunk along the grain, and the surface of the resulting board was made smooth by using an adze, which was a tool similar to an axe having an arch-shaped sharpened blade at right angles to the long handle.

The Adze

To use it, you stand astride or on the piece of wood and chop between your feet, a dicey job if you were recovering from a late night and had bare feet or were wearing sandals. But as Saws improved and could be made longer, the Pit Saw was invented to saw trees into baulks or planks. Using it involved digging a deep pit and placing trestles resting on baulks across the top of the pit, after which, the tree to be sawn was rolled on to the trestles and fastened in place. If a large tree was too big to be easily transported to an existing saw pit, one would be dug alongside the tree. The Pit would be roughly a six-foot cube and was manned by two men, one in the pit and one standing on top of the tree, the bottom man pulled the saw down for the cutting stroke, and his mate on top then pulled it back up on the return non-cutting stroke and prepared it for the next cutting-down stroke, making sure that to obtain a straight cut, the saw followed the chalk line marked along the top of the trunk. It was a long and laborious job and purgatory for the man in the pit with little air and showers of sawdust. Maybe providentially, the main saw pit in Clevedon was situated in Old Church Road next to the Sawyers Arms, where some relief could be obtained during and at the end of a long day. When the Pit closed, the Town's second Police Station was erected on the site and remained there until its demolition in the 1960s allowed the newly constructed Great Western Road, to join Old Church Road near to the Cinema.

A Pit Saw working during WW2.

When the Town saw pit in Old Church Road closed and the Sawyers Arms lost their best customers, local businesses in the Town transferred their custom to William's saw pit where a regular supply of sawn timber was available. This consisted mainly of locally grown hardwood timbers such as Elm, Oak, Ash, etc. as softwood was mostly imported from North America or the Baltic States into Bristol, from whence it could be supplied to Clevedon by rail or cart, the latter using the tortuous road through Long Ashton and Nailsea, an alternative method of transport was by sea using small sailing vessels or barges, which unloaded their cargoes at the wharf at Clevedon Pill, but that was more expensive as it involved paying a toll to the Lord of the Manor who owned it, and occasionally, there was a further charge to the local Board (Council) if goods had to pass over their Town weighbridge in Lower Old Church Road.

Transporting logs in long lengths by road was very difficult as the roads in many places were only dirt tracks with few bridges that could carry heavily laden waggons, neither could the waggons or timber carriages easily enter woodlands to load, so the alternative for short distances was a 'Nib' carriage, basically an inverted U-shaped axle between two large wheels, which enabled one end of the tree to be raised into the air while the other end dragged along the ground, causing a fair bit of surface damage when they travelled along the unmade highway.

A Nib Carriage with a heavy log being pulled by three horses.

Towards the end of the nineteenth century, the age of the Machine had arrived and large stationary sawing machines came into existence, and that, together with the improvement in roads and Mechanical transport, enabled large and long logs to be brought to central places (Sawmills) where they could be sawn into usable-sized timbers. This started the rapid decline and disappearance of the 'on-site' Saw Pits and their replacement by newly designed mechanical machines manufactured from iron. But these were expensive and cost money, so William, realising that he was in danger of falling behind his competitors, gave the matter a lot of thought and decided that he must change his ways and seek a better way to cut a tree than by Pit-sawing, and obtained some brochures on iron sawing machinery made by Pickles, Ransome, Robinson, and others. Then despite his suffering from the small Victorian entrepreneur's problem of lack of money, he decided that Bandsaws were the thing of the future and that he had to have one and set about using his skills as a wheelwright, blacksmith, and carpenter to make his own machine.

The result was a forty-eight-inch Horizontal Bandmill made mostly from wood with some metal fittings and comprised two four-feet wooden wheels in a frame suspended on two vertical wooden pillars about six feet from the floor. A six-inch-wide thin steel saw band, toothed on one side, made by Monningers of London ran around the two wheels. The tree trunk was carried on a wooden trolley running on wooden rails which was pulled through the two pillars and the horizontally running saw blade by a hand windlass. Once the initial cut had been made, the tree was turned over on its flat side, and different-sized blocks were placed beneath it to obtain the required thickness of plank to be produced. The machine turned out to be a success, so he made a thirty-eight-inch vertical Band resaw for cutting the planks produced in the sizes and shapes he required. The saw had two wheels, one above the other, and was still being used by a carpenter in his Leagrove Road workshop in 1950. On both machines the wheel bearings were made from apple wood and the Saws were kept in place by keeping the wheels apart by tension, which was applied and maintained by a large weight sliding on lever, acting on a fulcrum.

His yard was behind his house at Devonshire Place in Old Street and was not over big, it included a large cart and waggon workshop, Blacksmith's Forge, Sawmills, paint shop, undertaker's emporium, and gunpowder store, which meant that there was not a great deal of room to spare. The machinery was driven by a very hardworking small steam engine, which generously produced both smoke and steam in equal quantities. The sawdust created by the saws was dispersed liberally by the wind, which ensured that it was distributed fairly evenly over the near neighbourhood, so it was not all honey living near to any Shopland enterprise, but maybe the fact that all his neighbours were his tenants did help to avoid too many vociferous complaints. However, his machines worked, and he was very pleased when a pit saw was no longer needed, and the pit was filled in.

As he grew older, William gradually curtailed his work, only doing small jobs such as making the wooden bodies for the first of the Stephen motor cars made in Clevedon in 1897 and working his little Sawmill until his death in 1908 when his middle son, John, inherited it. But John was heavily involved in the building trade, and although being a skilled carpenter, he decided to close it down and concentrate his resources elsewhere. William's eldest son, Charles, had left Clevedon to build houses in the Cardiff and Newport areas of South Wales, and his youngest son, Edmund, was starting his own business by building two houses in Highdale Avenue, where the track led to Highdale Farm, and working a Forge behind 71 Old Street. To expand his enterprise and start to fulfil a long-held ambition, he had bought a Traction Engine with three trucks to start a Steam Haulage business, he was finding life quite difficult, money was hard to find, and he was therefore disinclined to start a new venture. Added to which, he was just married and had become a Methodist Local Preacher, which occupied most of his limited spare time.

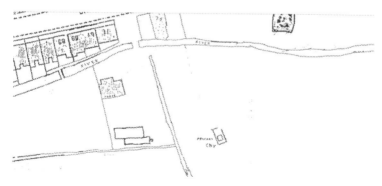

Edmund's Forge and First Sawmills (1897–1910).

The closing of William's Sawmill caused quite a stir and considerable disquiet amongst the other Builders in the Town as they were faced with the possibility of not having a local Timber supplier. As neither of Edmund's Brothers were interested in sawmilling, Edmund was approached to see if he would carry on his Father's business, but he was committed to his struggling Steam Road Haulage business and had all of his money tied up in that venture. That, together with the time required to start a new project, made him turn it down; added to which, his Brother John was not willing to lease him the premises at Devonshire Place, and in any case, their father's machinery was worn out.

However, the Builders were not prepared to let matters rest, and they continued to press him to change his mind. But the 1911 catastrophic industrial slump was looming. England was on the brink of a Political Revolution, which might sweep the Monarchy away, and finance was very tight, with the chances of borrowing capital to finance a new business almost impossible, so he kept saying "No". However, the continual pressure to start a Sawmill made Edmund think very hard about such a project, and eventually, to stop people banging on his door for an answer, he reluctantly decided to see if a Sawmill could be a viable proposition. So he erected some small sheds to house some sawmill machinery in the field behind his Old Street house, which had once been the Town Fair Field and Public Rubbish Dump.

He then journeyed to Bristol and bought an elderly second-hand reciprocating frame saw from the Victoria Wagon Company, though he still had no engine to drive it unless he took his Traction Engine off the road, which would cut off a profitable way to make money. However, Providence provided a solution when a retired builder, Thomas Hill, saw Edmund's predicament and, realising his financial plight, came to see him and said that as he was retiring, Edmund could have his steam engine, saw bench, mortar mill, and other tools and plant for fifty pounds if he would restart a Sawmill. Payment of the money would be treated as an indefinite loan, should the venture fail, the machinery could be returned to Mr Hill at no cost, or if it should succeed, the fifty pounds could then be paid out of any future profit when it was convenient for Edmund to do so.

Running a Haulage concern and Building Houses were quite demanding tasks and adding a Sawmill made it quite a struggle, especially as everything had to run on a financial shoestring, hoping that nothing would go wrong. It involved a great deal of hard work and very long hours as running and servicing a fully working Traction Engine could take up to twenty-two hours a day with maintenance at weekends. New staff had to be employed for the Sawmill, and fortunately, the various machines and their operators worked successfully together, enabling the small enterprise to survive and make a small profit. He was also able to develop a relationship with Lalonde Bros and Parham, who were Furniture Removers at Weston, and they agreed to give him some local jobs, and so Removals became another string to his bow.

Large quantities of oil were being bought from the First Anglo-Russian Oil Company (later Vacuum Oil Co. and ESSO) and Snowdrift Lubricants to maintain the Steam Engines, but motor cars were beginning to appear, and Edmund was persuaded to put in a Petrol Pump to sell Russian Oil Products petrol at ten old pence per gallon (4p). It was the second petrol pump to be installed in the Town as his friend Richard Stephens, the carmaker, had installed one in 1900 in the Triangle. Trade fluctuated in the lean years before the Great War, and there were several very bad winters when the frozen roads made it impossible for the steel-wheeled traction Engines to travel or keep the mill supplied with timber.

Borrowed Team of horses pulling a loaded Timber Carriage

When this happened, the firm had to borrow horses to haul timber in, but sometimes that method failed, and it was only Firewood and Coal sales that kept the enterprises afloat. But after a long while, things became relatively solvent, and enough money was made to repay Mr Hill in 1914, just before the Nation entered into the Great War. But best of all, the Bank Manager would still talk to him and help when times were good or bad.

In 1914, Edmund was elected to the Clevedon Urban District Council and put into place a policy of never selling anything to the Authority so that his motives could not be misunderstood. That policy is still enforced today, and the only things ever sold to local Councils are things which they have been unable to obtain elsewhere, e.g. Elm Fenders up to thirty feet in length and fourteen-inch square, which were needed to protect the Pier when the steamers tied up at the pier head in rough weather. When they were supplied, they had to be trundled to the end of the pier on rollers.

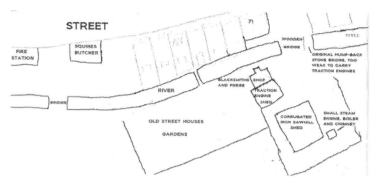

Sawmill c. 1910. *Guessing L–R*: Sam Coles, George
Newton, Boy and Carter not known.

Interior showing original Steam engine see three balls on
Governor behind boy, Who is the "phantom' soldier?

The commencement of the Great War in 1914 was a cataclysmic happening that altered the World, England, and Shopland's Sawmills forever. The Government removed the Owners' control over their mills by virtually nationalising all existing Sawmills in 1915 and placing Area Managers to have oversight, management, and the final say in the running of all of the sawmills in the kingdom. A nominal rent was then paid to the owner for the use of the machinery and the site. In North Somerset, a retired grocer was placed in charge, and he endeavoured to ensure that all the Sawmills under his authority were run on similar lines to a large grocers shop. According to Edmund, he knew nothing about the Timber Trade or sawmilling and less about man management, a combination which inevitably led to a major confrontation between them. A further complication was that the Government ordered that the mill should house and employ twenty Portuguese soldiers who had been brought to England when the Portuguese Army in France had refused to continue serving under the British Army General Staff. Hutted accommodation was erected for them in the Yard, and the Town set about learning Portuguese.

After a little exploration of the wartime Legislation, Edmund found that there was a loophole that permitted new Sawmills to be started and that they would be outside the authority of the National Timber Control. So he told the Controller that he was welcome to have the Old Street Mill, and as long as the rent was paid on time, he could do with it as he pleased, because Edmund was starting a new and smaller Mill in Parnell Road. He then decamped with his most reliable staff and set up a new small mill using second-hand machinery which had seen better days. The rent paid by the Government for the Old Street Mill was a pittance, and the new mill made very little money, but as it was subsidised by the Haulage business, it survived, earned Edmund a living, and kept a nucleus of trained labour together until the Timber control was disbanded in 1919 and the Old Street Mill premises were returned.

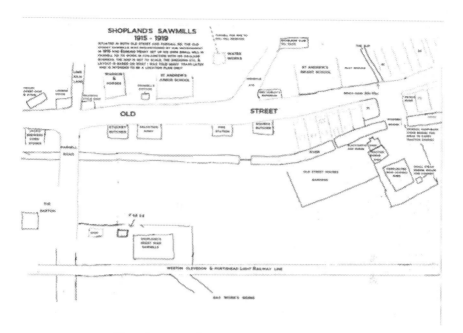

<u>Plan showing the two wartime Sawmills.</u>

Unfortunately, there was no compensation paid by the Government to finance replacing the worn-out machinery and dilapidated shedding that was handed back when the War had finished. To replace it all needed a great deal of capital, so Edmund sat down with his son Bert, who had returned from fighting on the Western Front in France, to decide their future, but it was not really a consultation or coming together of agreeing minds as Edmund was his own man and was used to making the decisions. His son would have rather given up the Sawmilling and concentrated on the Haulage side of the business as this could be combined with his real love, that of being a farmer. He also thought it would be best to move from Clevedon, but Edmund was adamant that housebuilding combined with sawmilling was still financially viable and the way forward; he also refused to leave Clevedon because of his Chapel and Council commitments. So the decision was made to continue with Sawmilling and the Building side of the Business with Edmund managing them and Timber buying and Bert concentrating on General

Haulage and keeping the Mill supplied with round Timber. When the ex-servicemen returned in 1919, there was a great deal of unemployment in England as many of their jobs had been filled by others during the War, but fortunately, with the new expansion, the Firm was able to take back all its former men and a few others as well.

All his early business records would have been handwritten into leather-bound ledgers using an ordinary pen and ink, as were letters when it was necessary to correspond with others using plain sheets of paper and they may have taken note of the famous advertisement for Fountain Pens, with their reservoir of ink contained within them, which said, 'The Swan, the Owl and the Waverly Pen. Came as a boon and a blessing to men.' After a while, he was able to afford letterheads printed by his friend George Hancock of Kenn Road, and that would have marked a big and confident step forward into the World of Commerce for Edmund and would have meant dispensing with the services of the telegram and the telegraph boy on his bike, for urgent and important messages.

Early in the 1920s, the local Elton Estate was subjected to a large Death Duty Bill, which resulted in much of the land and buildings that they owned in Clevedon having to be sold to raise the money to pay it. Included in the Sale were some fields around the Mill in Old Street which Edmund was able to purchase, and their acquisition meant that there could be a back entrance to the Mill from Parnell Road. The Firm could now expand and have a new approach to sawmilling by investing in the latest and most modern machinery, new sheds, and new carpenter's shop and creating a skilled workforce. So when the plan was finally decided, another visit was made to the Bank Manager. The Miles Estate at Walton in Gordano was also in the process of cutting back, and one of the young manservants, Gilbert, was dismissed and came to work as a Timber haulier. Upon leaving the Manor, he was given a redundant 'suit of tails' complete with a top hat as a parting gift. As he had nothing else to wear to work in his new job, his mother made sure he wore the gifted suit every day, and this pleased my Father greatly as anyone having any complaints addressed them to the 'immaculately attired Gentleman in Charge', i.e. Gilbert, who had carefully been briefed to say that he would have to pass them on to Mr Shopland at Clevedon when he returned to the Mill, thus absolving my Father from answering or deciding on awkward problems that arose.

Two other large Estates in the area were also affected by Death Duties, and they were the Smythes at Ashton Court and the Smythe-Piggotts at Brockley Hall. Both were forced to sell most of their large land holdings in North Somerset, but before doing so, they cashed in on the standing Timber, and Shoplands bought the Timber on Tickenham Hill and Worlebury Hill at Weston-super-Mare, plus some at Cleeve. Most of the trees in the woods were growing on steep slopes where the Traction Engines were unable to go, so to extract the felled timber from where it fell and take it to loading bays meant the re-employment of horses, and the result was three carthorses and a pony living in the stables until around 1936.

'Dragging out' on Tickenham Hill, part of the Smythe Estate.
Carriage and Engine. Carrige has skids attached,
ready to roll tree up on to it.

At this time, Clevedon was served by two railway systems—The Great Western, which was part of the National Rail Network, and a local Light Railway line, the Weston, Clevedon, and Portishead Light Railway Company (WC. & PR), which was unusually running on a standard gauge track similar to the National Network. The Light Railway track ran along the side of the Sawmills, and negotiations were made with the Company to install a Siding into the sawmills to deliver the trees directly into the yard. The Company was asked if it would bring the trees to Clevedon, which would save time and expense of road Haulage, it agreed, and the siding was installed, subject to the understanding that there would be a working access to the GWR National railway system as that would mean that sawn timber could be loaded into the railway waggons in the yard and save its having to be taken to the Station in Clevedon by lorry. Unfortunately, the connection to the GWR never came about, and the siding was removed in the late thirties after a bitter dispute over who should pay for its installation and use.

Light Railway train by New Street on the way to
Clevedon Station from Portishead. Just having passed
the Sawmills, which is behind the last waggon.

The local Light Railway was part of a scheme by a Colonel Stephenson to create a National Light Railway Empire in the British Isles, and the line joined Weston-super-Mare, Clevedon, and Portishead, having its main facilities and workshops based in Clevedon. It was not entirely solvent at times, and its rolling stock had, in the main, been items made redundant by other Railways. But it persevered and lasted until the start of the Second World War, when bankruptcy forced it to close, and most of its engines, waggons, carriages, and rails left the Town as scrap iron, soon afterwards, the track was removed and everything melted down to make arms to fight Hitler.

Plans for the new post Great War Mill included a larger Steam Engine to drive the extra Machinery as the old Engine would be underpowered and had seen better days, as had the Boiler, so when it was found that the local Water Company was selling a fairly new large Lancashire Boiler, a deal was done, and it was hauled from Tickenham and installed in a new purpose built Boiler House complete with a forty-foot chimney.

To maintain a supply of clean water for the boiler, a pump was installed near to a newly dug well which had been sunk adjacent to the river. To provide power for the Mill, a second-hand 150-hp Nealton and Haigh cross compound horizontal steam engine was purchased in Newcastle under Lyme.

Most of the mill engine came to Clevedon by rail, but the driving wheel was too large to pass through any railway tunnel and consequently had to come by road, hence, the deal included the purchase of a Burrell traction engine named Gladstone and a venerable timber carriage. Bert and two other ex-servicemen from the Great War and young Elliot Cole were sent to fetch the wheel to Clevedon, and it took five days and nights to complete the task, during which they never left the engine, living and sleeping alongside it. Their rations consisted of hard-boiled eggs and bread, which supposedly upset Elliot's digestive system, as he claimed many years later to have been egg-bound for life and spent a small fortune on a lifetime's purchase of anti-constipation remedies. The old Mill shedding was removed and replaced by two new sheds built side by side on brick pillars with ridge type roofs covered by tiles. In the front of the yard facing Old Street, a three ton, forty foot span overhead hand-operated gantry crane was erected and covered with a corrugated iron roof based on half-round timber trusses, which had roofed a WW1 wartime hangar on an airfield near Gloucester.

Harold Cole was appointed to maintain the boiler and the new engine, a task which involved firing the boiler four times a day, twice at night, and shovelling nearly a ton of coal a day if the Mill was working hard. Harold was also the keeper of the hours and was responsible for blowing the steam Hooter, which marked the start, end, and breaks in the working day. For that, he was issued with a new watch which was checked daily by Edmund. Tom Francis, in his Carpenter's shop, was the official

Timekeeper and kept the little board with its individual hanging named copper discs, which showed who was at work, late, or absent.

1924 — Main Drive Wheel for new Steam Engine.
Sixteen-foot diameter on sixteen-foot Shaft.
Burrel Gold Medal Tractor 'Gladstone' has just brought
the wheel from Newcastle under Lyme.
L–R: Boy 'a' Mapstone, Wilf Chard, E. H. Shopland,
H. W. Shopland, Bill Gibson, Elliot Cole.

Inside the mill, the gantry fed logs to the new sixty-inch Horizontal Bandmill bought from Haighs of Oldham, and a small derrick crane removed the sawn timber after it had been cut; the new machine considerably speeded up the sawing process and, through using thin saws, reduced the wastage on each cut, e.g. an eighth-inch cut instead of a quarter of an inch taken out by the blade of the old Frame saw. This saving, combined with the fast sawing, greatly contributed to the productivity and profitability of the Mill and was probably one of the main reasons for the Firm surviving the 1930s depression. Below is the purchase order for the Haigh Bandmill for £1671, which was a major financial outlay, something which was agonised over for a long time. I can only guess at the comparative cost today, and I suspect that it would be horrendous.

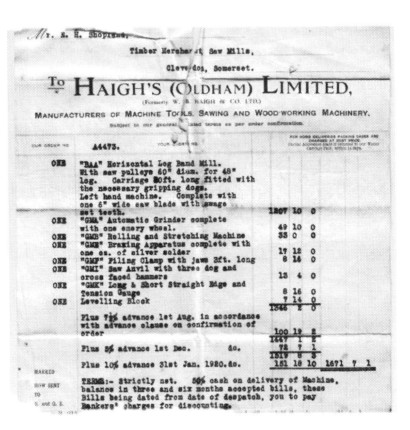

Invoice for Haigh Bandmill

Edmund and typical large Elm Butt 1940

Sawmill interior before 1914

Haigh—Large Elm butt for coffin board, 'burr' lump on top
will be sawn off complete and then sent away for veneer.
Note original Old Yard Office window in rear, which was later
to become the Firm's Wartime Fire-watching HQ, c. 1930.

Haigh Bandmill cutting Elm Coffin Board. L-R. H Cole HWS. EHS.

Haigh cutting African Baulk. Wedges being driven in to save saw from pinching. Log squared by hand in Africa using an adze, c. 1956.

Behind the Bandmill was a forty eight inch circular Rack bench for further breaking down the timber produced by the Bandmill and cutting small logs, also included was a thirty-six-inch circular saw, but there was one major problem which was in common with most factory practices that all of the power for the belt-driven machines came from the steam engine through pulleys on a central shaft, which limited the layout of the mill. There also was the fact that with no extraction system, the saw pits had to be emptied by hand, sometimes two or three times a day, which was a very time-consuming effort. The lack of a mechanical Fan Extraction Unit was mainly because it was not seen how to stop the sawdust from being blown into the neighbouring house gardens, something which might have upset them, though there was also the difficulty of keeping the machine pits dry as there was a high water table on the site. The main products produced were hardwood timbers for coffin boards, furniture, railway sleepers, and waggon repair timbers and general timber needed in the locality. Softwood for building would still be purchased from the Bristol Importing Merchants such as Taylor & Low Bros, May & Hassell, Heber Denty, and others.

After WW1, there was a great increase in the use of tin plate to make containers to preserve food, the plate was produced in South Wales and mostly shipped out of Lydney. To ease handling and transporting the sheets of plate, they were packed into shallow wooden trays or boxes, which had to be produced in large numbers at a very cheap price, so they were mostly made by using up otherwise waste wood. To speed up the production of Box boards for the tray bottoms, a James automatic circular saw box board cutting machine using a swage saw was purchased, and this maintained a constant supply of boards for the box makers, who, during the day, were mostly young boys and, at night, men who wished to earn some extra money by doing 'piecework' overtime.

STANDARD STATIONARY UNDERDRIVEN MORTAR MILL.
(ARE ALSO SUPPLIED OVERDRIVEN.)

The above is reproduced from a photo of our 7' Standard Underdriven Mortar Mill. (8' and 6' Mills are exactly the same design, except no Friction Rollers under Pan (not required).

No special foundation is required ; simply laid on four timber baulks (or railway sleepers). There is no Foundation Holding-down Bolts required, as its own weight keeps it in position.

These Mills are fitted with our Special Self-Lubricating Step.

We make these Mills in sizes from 5' to 9'. For Spare Part information, see Page twenty.

Size Mill	Rollers		Weight		Total Weight	Size of Pulleys	Horse Power Required	Speed, Revolutions per Minute	
	Dia.	Width	Mill	Parts				Pan	Shaft
			T. C. Q.	T. C. Q.	T. C. Q.		B.H.P.		
5'	2' 9"	12"	1 4 0	2 1 0	3 5 0	24" x 5½"	8	30	128
6'	3' 6"	14"	1 14 0	3 1 0	4 15 0	,,	10	27	134
7'	3' 6"	16"	2 6 0	3 15 0	6 1 0	,,	14	24	134
8'	3' 6"	18"	2 12 0	5 2 0	7 14 0	,,	16	21	134
9'	3' 6"	20"	2 14 0	5 10 0	8 4 0	,,	22	19	142

Typical Mortar Mill as supplied by Samsons of Malago Vale in Bristol.

As Housebuilding expanded in the area, a new Mortar Mill was bought from Sampsons Iron Founders in the Malago at Bedminster, and this was installed together with a lime pit where quarried lime was slaked with water to make lime putty, which was an essential ingredient in the making of mortar together with the clinker ash from the large boilers in the district, including the two waterworks at Tickenham and Chelvey, the Laundry, Keene's Brick works, the Gas works, and sometimes the Nail Factory and Brick works at Portishead. Old bricks and tiles were also added and the mixture ground until it was a thick bluish-coloured paste, after which, the finished product was mainly sold to the local builders at 16/- per pony cartload (roughly fifteen hundredweight) delivered locally, though there were a few other customers who came from Yatton, Nailsea, Pill, and Portishead. Additional Yard activities were Oak Gate and Wheelbarrow making in the Carpenter's shop by Tom Francis. Sometimes the Blacksmith Forge was lit for Edmund to mend something for a special friend, and a Public Weighbridge to weigh up to twenty tons was installed.

The new approach to Sawmilling and the creation of larger Sawmills also necessitated changes in the provision of extra round timber for the Mill, which in turn meant travelling further distances to obtain it. But through the Firm having a policy of felling the timber and removing it on the same day, there was an effective ban on anything outside a thirty mile radius from Clevedon as horses and Steam Locomotives were too slow. There were not many mature woodlands in North Somerset, and those in South Gloucestershire served the Bristol Home-Grown Timber Sawmills such as Toogoods, Gillams, Chapmans, and a few others on the outskirts of the City, so most of the supply for Clevedon came from hedgerow Elms from as far afield as Bruton and Taunton, with the main number coming from the Wedmore, Street, and Wells areas. The distance factor also applied to the sale of the products as the local market was swamped. Customers were found in Bristol and further afield, such as Swansea, Liverpool, and the Midlands. But selling this far from home involved having the goods delivered by rail and paying selling agents a commission to find customers and collect the money; such agents included Brockley Timber Co., a local firm run by Mr Owen, Tim Hasnip, John Neath, and Graham Tripp, all of whom were friends, Taylor Maxwell's of Bristol and others. But using their services reduced profits. However, there were a few direct contacts such as H. & J. Sankey of Bootle in Liverpool who bought a lorryload of Elm Coffin Boards each week and Llewellyn Davies of Briton Ferry in South Wales who took a railway waggon load weekly.

Coffin boards were sold in sets—one top board and one bottom board, both twenty four inches and wider, and sold sawn 'through and through' (i.e. with bark on edges), three side boards (one to make ends), square edged fourteen inches and wider. All were six feet-six inches and longer and normally three quarters of an inch thick, though a special high-quality coffin would have boards planed to finish at an inch in thickness. Tops and sides had to be knot and blemish-free as that was what the customer and their friends would see and judge the quality of the coffin by, though occasionally a knot in the top board of a coffin could be covered by the brass nameplate. The bottom board could be rougher as it was out of sight. Oak coffins were rare and usually only made for the very wealthy, though sometimes a compromise on cost would be made by using sweet chestnut, which, when planed and polished, was almost indistinguishable to oak to the casual onlooker. New transport for the extra distance haulage had to be found, so a gradual change was made to petrol lorries, which were at first solid tyre ex–WD AECs and Albions from the Great War, later, these were changed for pneumatic-tyred vehicles such as a thirty-hundredweight Dennis, and two three-ton Bristol tankers which had been bought from the Shell Mex Petrol Co. for £25. Their petrol carrying tanks were removed and replaced by homemade winches, which enabled them to be used as timber haulage tractors. Their top speed varied between fifteen and twenty miles per hour and increased the radius of timber purchases to about forty miles. Sadly, this vehicle reorganisation meant a parting of the ways with the more elderly carters who could or would not adapt and deal with any vehicle that did not respond quickly to the verbal command of 'Whoa', So eventually the only horse-drawn vehicle left in the Sawmills was a small pony cart used for local firewood deliveries, and it usually had a boy in charge.

A Terrible Worldwide Slump started in 1928 and, together with Mass Unemployment, virtually brought the Country to a halt, and it lasted until preparations were made for the Second World War in 1938. The slump closed many businesses which bought poverty and despair to many homes and caused many people to have to beg in the streets to survive, and their state was poignantly and tragically summed up by an American song of the time which asked the question, 'Buddy, can you spare a dime?' The recession also had a dramatic effect on the Sawmills as although there was trade, money had disappeared, and at times, there was little hope of being paid for the work you had done. This was not a deliberate ploy by customers to avoid paying but came about because the financial ground on which they stood was changing day by day, as their customers often defaulted and could not pay, resulting in your customers closing and disappearing in the short time from when they had last spoken to you, placed and received their order.

William Staddon had been apprenticed to one of my Grandmother's brothers who had been a partner in Grace and Hayes, Timber importers in Bristol. After leaving them, he had set up a thriving business importing hardwood logs from North America to be sawn to provide timber for vehicle body building, and in the late twenties, he had come to live in Clevedon. He was looking for someone to saw his trees who had space to dry and season the cut boards afterwards, so he came to see Edmund. They hit it off and started working together. Most of the logs were imported or came from other parts of the British Isles and arrived at Clevedon Station by rail where they were unloaded by a hand-operated railway crane. After sawing, the boards were taken to the stacking ground by an internal light railway. It was a very happy partnership, and his son Clifford often accompanied Shopland's Cricket team when they played their annual fixture at Kingston Seymour and other local villages, provided both his lady friend and the motorbike were agreeable.

Added to the woes of the slump was a successful move by the large oil Companies to persuade the Government to alter the way in which commercial vehicles were taxed by changing from a fixed annual fee to a charge based on the vehicle's unladen weight. The reason behind their action was to preserve their petroleum monopolies and profits and prevent the long-term development of the steam engine, which could have eclipsed its petrol equivalent; their success immediately placed steam vehicles at a great disadvantage as their weight was considerably more than their petrol contemporaries. The result was that Steam vehicles were forced off the road and scrapped, again leading to a considerable loss of jobs. Their arbitrary demise caused great financial hardship and problems for many small businesses, as at a stroke, their main financial assets were devalued completely. There was no money available to fund any alternatives, and this was probably the main reason for Shopland's retirement from long-distance road haulage, a bad move for the family as the War and the subsequent peace saw a great expansion in road haulage and many fortunes made when the Road Haulage Industry was first nationalised by the State and then denationalised. And yet again, there was the trauma of laying off long-serving and loyal labour, knowing that there was no alternative employment available.

Trade was difficult throughout the thirties. Building virtually ceased, and Edmund was stuck with twelve new houses that he had built and could not sell in New Street because no one could raise the £25 deposit, so in the end, they had to be let at very low rents, and this caused a major Family Financial crisis, so another visit had to be made to the Westminster Bank where the manager advanced a loan of over twenty thousand Pounds on a handshake and virtually no security. There was no time limit on the loan, and it was finally paid off at the end of the War. Timber prices were low and paying work scarce, but the Firm struggled on and was helped by the attitude of its employees who knew that money was hard to find for wages and never asked for an increase as they knew it would mean someone losing their job.

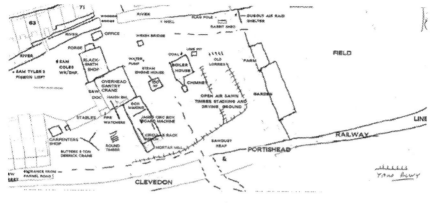

Site Plan

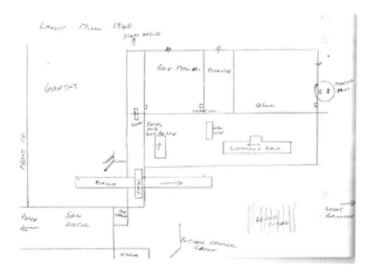

Interior Plan of main Mill
Machines driven by overhead shafting and flat belts.

From 1938 to the early 1940's was a calamitous time for the Sawmills and the Family as three valued members of the workforce were killed in succession in separate incidents whilst at work. Samuel Genge was a Timber Feller and was killed in a car accident when on his way to fell some trees at Mark. The second tragedy happened in the Clevedon Railway Yard when Harry Scribbins was killed when some railway sleepers being loaded into a railway truck by crane, slipped out of the chain sling and fell on to him. The third event was almost the saddest as it involved a teenager Charley Martin who fell off the cab step of the Bristol Tractor as it was passing over rough ground, the rear wheels of the tractor ran over him and he later died in hospital. It was a devastating blow and but for a deep sense of duty that in a time of peril everyone should help the Country by not rocking the boat, Edmund and Bert would have closed the business and gone their separate ways. However, with a second major war imminent trade improved and more money became available, and when War was declared in 1939, Shoplands decided to buckle down and do their bit. But it came as a big shock when Factory Hooters and Whistles were banned, and for the first time for nearly a hundred years, Shoplands no longer proclaimed their version of the time of the day to all and sundry throughout the Town. Timber was of great importance to the War effort, and The Government again established a Timber Control Ministry which granted licences for timber buying and selling, so ensuring that timber was only supplied to Industries directly involved in the War effort. In addition, they sent Inspectors to make spot physical checks on licences and stocks, with draconian fines and stiff penalties for any infringements. Sometimes prison sentences could be imposed for breaking or ignoring the control system, but having learnt a hard lesson in WW1, the Ministry played no part in the individual management of firms and left that to the existing owners. Most timbers were controlled, though there were a few exceptions, such as Elm and Oak, where it was to be used as coffins. This also applied to Poplar, which, as it was light in weight, when seasoned, was used to make coffins for deceased American Servicemen being returned to the USA by plane.

Wartime Controls

Below are some of the myriad number of Forms that bedevilled the War effort and introduced the post-war scourge of 'pen and button pushing' civil servants and public employees.

AGREEMENT "A" N° A.826.

THE ANNEXE REFERRED TO IN THE AGREEMENT
HOME GROWN HARDWOODS FOR NATIONAL STOCK

1. All Timber covered by the attached Specification to be winter felled.

2. All thicknesses to be full off saw. The percentage against each thickness indicates proportion required in cubic feet.

3. Through and through Plank to be Log selection and measured in accordance with the custom of the Trade.

4. Lengths will be accepted in half feet, and widths of Square-Edged material in half inches. All the material cut against the Square-Edged Specifications must be well manufactured with parallel edges.

5. Oak and Spanish Chestnut - not less than 50% to be Square-Edged material.

6. The quantity of Square-Edged Beech, Items 10, 11 and 12 originally required, having been reduced, Sawmillers may increase the quantity of through and through Beech Plank, Item No.9, to the extent of the uncompleted portion of the Square-Edged material contracted for.

7. The quantity of second quality accepted must not exceed in cubic feet the quantity of first quality material.

8. All material to be subject to inspection, either at the producing Mill or on delivery to Timber Control Central Depots.

9. The price shown against each Specification is subject to the increases permitted to certified Port-City and Town Mills.

Signed on behalf of the Sawmiller

. . . .

Signed on behalf of the Ministry of Supply

. . . . Chief Assistant
(Timber Control Department)

(13/6/48)

9.BEECH
1st quality butts
8' & up in length.
14" & up quarter girth,T.O.B.
To be straight,sound,clean
and practically free from
knots or other defects.
Allowance to be made in
measure of plank for defects.
Sawn through and through to
the following thicknesses:-

40%	1"
10%	1½"
20%	1¾"
20%	2"
10%	2½"

Price - 1½" & up 5/-d cu.ft.
Under 1½" 6/-d "

10.BEECH
1st quality square edged
6' & up in length,averaging
8' or better.
6" & up in width,averaging
8" or better.
Clear,flat,free from splits,
shakes,wane and centre.
Sawn to the following
thicknesses:-

20%	1"
10%	1½"
10%	1¾"
40%	2"
5%	2½"
15%	3"

Price - 6/6d per cu.ft.

11.BEECH
1st quality square edged
3'-5'6" in length.
4" & up in width,averaging
7" or better.
Clear,flat,free from splits,
shakes, wane and centre.
Sawn to the following thicknesses:

30%	1"	30%	2"
20%	1¼"	10%	3"
10%	1½"		

Price - 5/6d per cu.ft.

12.BEECH
2nd quality square edged
5' & up in length,
averaging 7' or better.
6' & up in width,admitting
20% 4"-5½", averaging 8"
or better.
Admitting small sound knots
not exceeding 1" diameter.
To be flat, free from wane
and centre.
Sawn to the following
thicknesses:-

30%	1"
20%	1¼"
10%	1½"
30%	2"
10%	3"

Price - 5/-d per cu.ft.
less 10%.

13.ELM
1st quality butts
10' & up in length.
15" & up quarter girth,
T.O.B.
To be straight,clean and
sound mild timber,admitting
a few defects at the
discretion of the Inspector.
Allowance to be made in
measure of plank for
defects.
Sawn through and through
to the following thicknesses:-

25%	¾"
35%	1"
10%	1¼"
20%	1½"
10%	2"

Price - 1½" & up 4/3d
per cu.ft.
Under 1½" 5/3d
per cu.ft.

3/6/150

```
Telephones:                    MINISTRY OF SUPPLY,
        Bristol (36861.          TIMBER CONTROL DEPARTMENT,
                 (37041.          Clifton Down Hotel,
Telegrams:                        Bristol, 8.
     Timberhead, Bristol.

Department III, Branch 6.             15th August, 1941.


Messrs.E.Shopland & Son,
Old Street,
Clevedon,
Som.


Dear Sirs,

          Home Grown Hardwoods - National Stock.

          I am directed by the Timber Controller to refer
to the Provisional Order placed with you by your Area
Officer to supply a quantity of Home Grown Hardwoods
for National Stock.

          Two copies of the Agreement are enclosed, one of
which has been completed by the Ministry of Supply,
which should be signed and retained by you.  The
other should be signed by you where indicated and
returned to the Ministry of Supply, Timber Control
Department, Department III Branch 6, Clifton Down
Hotel, Bristol 8, without delay.

                    Yours faithfully,


                    G. P. W. EDWARDS
                    Chief Assistant
                    Branch 6, Dept.3
```

In the confusion at the start of the conflict, the emphasis was on building up the Armed Forces by the creation of The National Service Act, which called up men to serve in the Armed Forces. But no provision was made for the exemption of those key workers essential to keep the Country running and make armaments, so there were many 'paper' battles fought with officialdom to reclaim exempt worker who had been wrongly called up. The remaining workforce was strictly controlled and directed to wherever it was needed.

Below are typical letters for a Top Sawyer who had been wrongly called up and confirmation of his discharge from the Armed Forces.

Chewton Mendip,
Nr. Bath.
6.1.40.

Messrs. E.H. Shopland & Son,
The Saw Mills,
Old Street,
Clevedon.

Dear Sir,

Re Gnr. YOUDE R.J. No. 2022968

I am directed to acknowledge receipt of your letter of 4.1.40 relating to the above named Gunner.

Your remarks are noted and appreciated, but application for this man's release must be submitted to the Ministry of Supply, Timber Control Department (Labour) 2/7 Elmdale Road, Bristol, 8 who must in their turn submit this application through the proper channels for consideration by the appropriate committee at the War Office, who will send us instructions as to the action they wish taken regarding Gnr. Youde's release.

I am,
Sir,
Your obedient Servant,

Commanding 23rd. Light A.A. Regiment RA

FORESTRY COMMISSION,
(Timber Supply Department),
2/7, Elmdale Road,
BRISTOL.8.

E.46.

File 500/ ᵃ/

Dear Sirs,

With reference to your application
for the release from Military Service

(R. F. Youde)

whose release I understand has been
authorised, I shall be glad to know
whether or not he has returned to your
employ. ~~they have~~

Should the above man not have
returned, it would be of assistance if
you would forward me the address of
present unit. Also please inform me
of rank and regimental number, if this
has not already been forwarded.

Yours faithfully,

[signature]

for Commissioner (Labour)

Messrs E. H. Shopland & Son,
Clevedon Saw Mills,
Clevedon.
Somerset.

Exemption Notice for another employee.

NATIONAL SERVICE ACTS.

MINISTRY OF LABOUR AND NATIONAL SERVICE,
DISTRICT MAN POWER BOARD,

10, PRIORY ROAD,

BRISTOL 8

1 3 NOV 1943 (Date).

Dear Sir(s)

Employee *Scribbins. E.*

Occupation *Tractor Driver* - N.S. Regn. No. *CLB 415*,

With reference to your application on form N.S. 300 for the deferment of calling-up of the above-named employee, I have to inform you that the District Man Power Board has decided to grant deferment until *May 12 - 1944*, after which date the employee will be regarded as available for calling-up for service or for transfer to other work.

You should retain this notification for production if required. Should the occupation of the employee change or the employee cease to be employed by you before the expiration of the period of deferment, you should complete the form below and return it to this office immediately.

Yours faithfully,

for District Man Power Board.

Notification to Ministry of Labour and National Service.

Through no fault of their own, Staddons, the other Timber Merchants in the Town, were badly affected by the War as there could be no importation of Timber from abroad, and consequently their trade virtually ceased, which was a major blow to the Sawmills and a loss of good friends and partners. Fortunately they were able to continue in business on the fringes of the Trade throughout the War and were able to resume their activities properly after 1945.

Lack of Imports affected all of the major Timber Importers, and to stay in business, they became involved in the Home-Grown Timber Trade, although they had large amounts of capital to invest, their lack of knowledge of the trade upset the market and caused quite a few complications for a while. Ivor Clarke of Clarks Wood Company in Bedminster came to see Edmund, and an arrangement was made for them to take the place of Staddons and supply a source of logs for the Mill to saw. The trees were hauled to the Mill from places as far afield as Cornwall and Devon mostly by Henry Giles of Bath, who started with elderly pre-war lorries, then ex–Ministry Unipowers, ex–WD Army

Quads, and later, new post-war Leyland Beaver Tractors and Articulated Vehicles.

When the Clark trees had been cut, a team of men was sent down from Bristol to stack the planks for them to dry, using a Thorneycroft lorry to transport them from the Mill to the stacking ground, which made the small yard light railway redundant, and it was removed. To speed up production by improving the method of supplying logs to the Bandmill, a Butters three-ton Derrick Crane with a sixty-foot jib was installed, and my Father Bert said that it might be best to call it a Nutter's crane as the only person prepared to work it was an ex–WW1 veteran from the trenches who was totally deaf, often failed to correctly interpret the frantic hand signals sent his way, and sometimes failed to react quickly to the problems caused by the crane being in an exposed position, which often resulted in any strong wind, making the jib act like a sail which would take over control of the slewing of the crane, scatter the workforce working beneath it, and lead to almost disastrous results.

As the volume of timber to be sawn increased, so did the need for sharp saws to cut it, and this resulted in having to invest in a new fully equipped Saw Doctor's shop in the new premises, and Charlie Warriner joined the Firm to take charge of it.

The Art of the Saw Doctor

The first saws used to cut Timber were straight-bladed and were sharpened and maintained by each individual Sawyer for his machine using a whetstone or later a hardened metal file. But in the mid 1800s, Steel manufacturing improved to allow the production of thin steel plate suitable for making circular saws, and these were introduced to the Timber Trade. Their appearance meant that someone had to be trained to service and maintain them as they have to be tensioned by hammering to make them cut straight and prevent them from bursting through centrifugal force when they rotate at high speeds, and in addition, their teeth have to be ground and set, so the profession of a Saw Doctor came into being at about the same time. Steel production improved and became capable of producing endless lengths of steel band down to a sixteenth of an inch in thickness and widths of up to ten inches wide. Steel strip to make bandsaw blades was supplied in large rolls and then cut into the required length to make an individual saw; after being cut to length, teeth were cut into one edge, and the ends of the band were chamfered and brazed together (soldered) to make a continuous band. Nowadays, the joints are simply butt-welded together.

On a Bandsaw, the blade runs on two pulleys which have slightly domed centres on their rims, the bandsaw is tensioned on either side, leaving an untensioned trip in its middle, which fits over the dome on the pulley and keeps the saw in place. This tension is created and maintained by skilful machine rolling and hand hammering, which also has to ensure that a straight back to stop the saw from running erratically is maintained on the edge opposite to the teeth. The teeth are spaced out and ground into shape, having their cutting point squeezed so that there are slight projections on either side of the tooth (the swage), which makes the cut a little wider than the metal strip and allows the hook to collect the sawdust and drop it into the gullet to remove the waste material (sawdust).

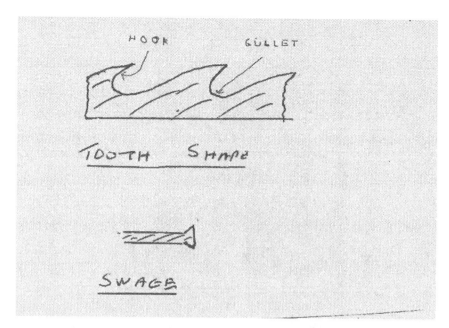

HOOK   GULLET

TOOTH   SHAPE

SWAGE

Illustration of tooth shape and top view of swaged tooth.

All these processes are highly skilled and only learnt after a long and arduous apprenticeship, and the maintenance of Bandsaws can be literally a matter of life and death should a band break through bad tensioning or a fault in making the join. Their accuracy in making straight cuts, together with their cutting life, measures and controls the profitability and long-term future of any Sawmill, so dependence on the skills of the Saw Doctor is essential for a Mill's survival, consequently, the good and competent Saw Doctor is always treated with great respect and paid accordingly.

Butters Jib crane working in Yard. Chimney and Court Woods in background. EHS in foreground. c. 1942

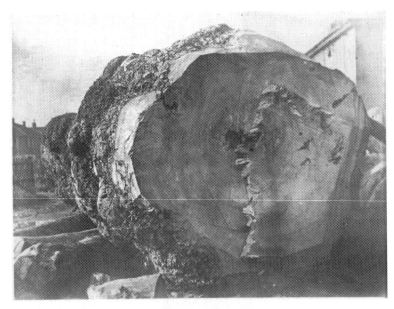

Tyntesfield Elm

**George Hartree X cutting 8ft. Diam. 'Tyntesfield'
Elm with Witte Saw. c.1947
George was a (WW1 veteran) who worked as a
boy for William Shopland before 1900,
then Edmund, Herbert & David – four generations.**

As prior to 1914 and the Great War, many of the younger lads working in the Mill had joined the local Territorial Army Unit to get some pocket money and a paid week's holiday at Annual Camp, so on the declaration of War in 1939, they were all called up and disappeared, leaving the Mill short of labour. To replace them, some local recruiting was done, and other men from outside Clevedon were directed in by Government decree as a part of their war work, but in many cases, the 'draftees' resented living in lodgings and working in a sawmills as the work was hard, dirty, and at times, cold and wet, added to which, the average age of those employed rose to over forty-five with a resulting lack of mobility and energy. Solving all of these problems meant that a great deal of retraining was necessary and resulted in a falling off in production and drop in earnings. Consequently, at times the Mill was not a very happy place, and it was only Bert's endless patience, together with his diplomatic and management skills, that kept things going.

Many essential supplies were rationed and in short supply, including coal for the Boiler, added to which in the latter's case, the best-quality coal from South Wales and had been reserved for Admiralty Warships. The nearest local source of coal was from a Colliery at Kilmersdon near Radstock, and the coal it supplied was of poor quality and when it was burnt, produced more clinker and ashes than heat. The debris clogged up the tubes of the boiler and resulted in a great deal of time being lost through extra cleaning and maintenance.

Now that bureaucracy, officialdom, and mindless interference had again entered business life in a large way, Edmund quickly realised that his Victorian attitude to Business and Employment was sadly out of date, so in view of the changing laws concerning employment, Factory Acts, and general litigation, he realised that he was not justified in shouldering the possible financial liabilities and penalties involved with running a business without adequate protection. So to solve the problem, he decided to form a limited Company with his son and one of his daughters, though he kept a majority of the shares so that he was still in charge, and so E. H. Shopland & Son (Clevedon) Ltd. came into being.

Telephone 107.   Established 1897.   Telegrams—"Shopland, Saw Mills, Clevedon."

E. H. SHOPLAND & SON (Clevedon) Ltd.

Directors: **English Timber Merchants,**
E. H. SHOPLAND
(Managing Director).   **Builders and Haulage Contractors,**
H. W. SHOPLAND
B. M. SHOPLAND   SAW MILLS, CLEVEDON.

Som.

M.   194

New Company Letterhead 1940

As the War continued, there were increasing shortages to contend with. High-Grade Steel became scarce, causing the quality of the saws to fall, which meant that they quickly lost their edge and had to be sharpened more often with inferior files. This meant that more time and production was lost, which soon became a major problem when Ministry deadlines could not be met. Petrol was rationed, and sometimes paraffin had to be added to vehicle petrol tanks to complete the journey home. A few brave souls converted their vehicles to burning sawdust in the absence of air to make gas, which provided limited power. New batteries and tyres for vehicles were non-existent, and many a truck had the white canvass showing on its tyres as it rolled along, possibly the revolving white canvass was a help in showing where the vehicle was in the blackout. Food was also severely rationed, though there was a small extra allowance for Manual workers in Heavy Industries, and the issue of a tea ration started the stopping for a 'tea break' ritual. New clothing was rarely available to citizens, so the workers' dress often consisted of First World War bits and pieces, pre-war suits, and even at times, sack bags and the occasional canvas apron.

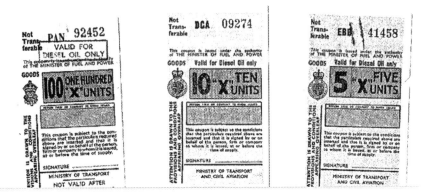

Petrol coupons in this case a 'unit' is one gallon.

Although Sawmilling was a reserved occupation which exempted the staff from full-time Military Service, there were still compulsory Wartime commitments to fulfil at night, either in the ARP, which involved patrolling designated streets looking for Black-out infringements and giving assistance to Householders in the event of an air raid, carrying Arms in the Home Guard to defend the Country if the Germans invaded, or serving in the National Fire Service fighting fires in the Blitz. All were uniformed and had an enforceable legal commitment.

Home Guard Call up Notice.

Also, during non-working hours, there was the chore of tending the allotment or garden to produce extra food to supplement the meagre ration allowance for the family. Fulfilling all these tasks meant that at times it was a very tired workforce that reported for work early in the morning. These factors, together with an unavailability of any spares to replace items that broke, made it very difficult to keep the aging machinery and worn-out lorries that had done yeoman service throughout the depression years continue working. Again, the consequent steady loss of production didn't sit well with official Government targets and predictions.

FIRE-WATCHING

In 1940, the Government decreed that all Industrial Premises should have persons on duty twenty-four hours a day to deal with any Fires caused by enemy action, and so 'The Fire-watchers' were created. In the Sawmills, men were working during the day for six days a week, so they were only needed for nights and Sundays. My Father and Grandfather covered daylight hours on Sundays, and others working in pairs were on duty throughout each night, i.e. from 10 p.m. to 6 a.m. the following day. The routine officially laid down was one hour watching and one hour off resting, but in the end, how it was done was left to those doing it as long as one was awake. For this, they were paid five shillings per night regardless of age or position in the Firm, and it must have been quite an art to select a compatible 'night companion' on a regular basis over several years from the same few staff you worked with during the day.

Gradually, the cost-cutting and 'make do and mend' measures of the depression years started coming home to roost and making themselves felt. Matters came to ahead late in 1943 when Shopland's Sawmill buildings gave up the fight, collapsed, and sank slowly to the ground amidst a rising cloud of thick dust. This was a major calamity, but the saving grace was that no one was hurt as fortunately, it was lunchtime and everyone was outside watching an aerial dogfight in the sky and hoping that the German Plane would be shot down, so no one really saw or realised what had happened until they turned to go back to work. The theory behind its collapse was that the continuous vibration from the Steam Engine and the belt shafting had, over the years, undermined the foundations of the brick pillars holding up the roof. Only the Bandmill and the Gantry remained in working order. Production zeroed, and labour was laid off. The Ministry became involved as they didn't want to lose Shopland's contributions to the War effort, so again, new plans had to be drawn up and special dispensations obtained to erect steel-framed buildings and more overhead cranage. And at the same time, the major decision was taken to change over from steam to electricity as the main source of power.

Moving from steam meant doing away with a central shaft line, and as each machine could now have an individual electric motor, it could be situated where it was needed most. After a short while, Electricity was found to be cheaper, cleaner, and more economical, with the first quarterly Bill being less than the monthly wage of the man in charge of the boiler. On the transport side, the two Bristol Tractors were working hard, and official permission was given to purchase two eight-ton Timber carriages made by Automower and Tasker. A converted Commer Furniture van took over the out-of-town deliveries. Firewood again became a very important item as coal was strictly rationed and sometimes unavailable. A lengthy customer list was compiled and gave rise to endless disputes as to who was next for their chumps, and Eddy Palmer and the little ex–Shell-Mex Dennis lorry were anxiously watched by ever so many waiting observers as they trundled round the Town making deliveries, everyone hoping that some of the chumps were theirs.

To maintain Public Morale the Government allowed Fairs, Circus's etc. to travel around the Country and whilst all of the Sawmill renovations were taking place a small travelling Circus visited Clevedon and set up its 'Big Top' (Tent) in the field next to the Sawmills. It's star attraction was an Elephant and after the last performance in the ring he decided that he did not wish to leave the Town and staged a sit down protest in the Mill Yard. This prompted a long debate about whether an Elephant would be of use working the yard handling smaller logs as it was long before the age of the forklift. Delicate negotiations were entered into with the Circus owner, a price was agreed and Jumbo nearly came to live in the old Stables. Why it never happened is not really known but maybe my Grandmother's observation that my Grandfather, clothed only in a skimpy loin cloth, perched on the animals head when acting as 'mahout' might look rather silly, influenced the final decision to manage without Jumbo.

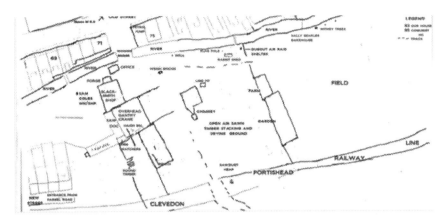

1944 - Site Plan of rebuilt New Mill with Overhead 5 ton Gantry Circular Rack Bench changed to Stenner 42" Band rack

Looking into Mill from new Gantry. Stenner 42" Rack bench and circular saw-bench. L-R- R Youde on saw bench. C.Wallis. c 1945.

Front Yard with Tasker carriage c.1944.

Teignmouth Road Gantry- unloading Bristol
Tractor & Tasker Carriage c. 1944

During the war, several small sawmills opened in the area, all having a minimal amount of machinery. One was at Wrington, another at Chewton Mendip, and others at Clapton in Gordano, Weston-super-Mare, and near to The Barrow Gurney water reservoirs. Locally, in 1941, a Mr E. Hayward came from Devon to Clevedon and started a mill powered by a traction engine in Coles Old Quarry in Holly Lane and delivered his sawn timber to the Clevedon GWR Station using a four-wheel trolley pulled by the largest carthorse ever seen in Clevedon, which was driven by Mrs Grigg. But they have all now been closed, and Mrs Griggs's horse Midget pensioned off.

Circular saw rack bench and Traction Engine
working in Hayward's Holly Lane Sawmills.
NB. No belt or saw guards.

When the War finished in 1945, there was great rejoicing and Trade increased, but many of the returning ex-servicemen did not want to go back to their mundane pre-war jobs, and that resulted in a surge of semi-trained people trying to do tradesmen's work with the inevitable drop in standards of workmanship. In the Mill, it again, as in 1919, meant a lot of retraining for former staff and detailed instruction for new employees, including Derek Pendar, who joined the Office Staff. Derek, a former trainee Solicitor's Clerk in London, as an eighteen-year-old Gunner had been evacuated at Dunkirk and, on demob, wanted to broaden his horizons. Greater volumes of timber were required to reconstruct the Country, and the contract sawing now included Imported Logs such as Obeche, Iroko, and Sapele from West Africa, many of which were landed at Avonmouth and Bristol Docks and had to be hauled to Clevedon. The firm had bought timber for many years from the small Estate owned by a millionaire, Sidney Hill, at Langford House near Churchill. Mr Hill was a bachelor without any immediate family, and when he died, he left instructions that the Estate was to be offered to Edmund for a nominal sum. This was again a chance to move the Sawmills from Clevedon, but Edmund turned it down for the same reasons as he had refused to move to Portbury House in 1918 and decided to modernise the Clevedon Mill and increase production. To do this, a forty-two-inch Stenner Band push saw replaced one of the circular saws, and a new sixty-inch Vertical Stenner Bandmill was bought in 1951. This was the last major decision concerning the future of the Sawmills with which Edmund was involved, as his wife died shortly after in 1953 and he quickly followed her in 1954.

African Log on Haigh Bandmill carriage.
L-r : HWS. H Cole. Above HC George Youde, Derek Pendar. C. 1947.

Three Generations of the Shopland Family in 1950.
Left- EHS. In crane DWS. Right HWS.

HWS and Foreign logs under gantry

Group in backyard back yard by New St. Houses.
L-R:- Back row –. Paddy Ransome. C Pearce. Unknown. Jack Ralph.
Middle row- G Youde. S Aldom. Eddy Palmer.
Front row - H Cole. R Youde. c.1946.

Group sitting on old wooden bridge outside 71 Old St.
L-r. Standing - Reg & George Youde. Sitting – Charles Watson. C
Pearce. H Cole. DWS. E Palmer. J Ralph (Saw Doctor) c. 1946

Oak Butt in fore-ground with New 3ton Gantry behind
photo taken from Teignmouth road. 1950.
New Stenner Head-rig to right of Gantry crane.

60" Stenner Bandmill Foundation,
L-r : Left of concrete mixer wooden builders
wheelbarrow made in yard Carpenter's Shop.
At Concrete Mixer - George Hartree with shovel & Ted Neath,
Wheel barrow L Mann, Spreading concrete DWS. Standing
watching EHS. In far corner- F Gibson. S Cole.

Stenner 60" Vertical Bandmill :- Loading side - Looking
out of Gantry towards New St. Houses

Stenner looking opposite way

Stenner:- Final Inspection Committee –L-R
David, Herbert and Edmund Shopland.

Stenner:- First trial cut L-R. Reg Youde. Stenner's Installation Fitter.

Stenner:- Ted Neath chopping Elm Butt to go under top pulley.

Stenner:- Cutting 6' diameter Obeche Log to 2" boards.
L – R, George Youde, DWS. Reg Youde (Sawyer), Harold Coles.

Edmund's death caused many problems as his estate had to be divided into three. The Sawmill was a large part of the Estate, and Bert's sisters wanted to leave part of their inheritance money in the business so that some of their family could work and help manage it, in particular, my cousin John Maggs and my Aunty Byrde's husband, Jack Kings. However, they were personalities who would find it hard to agree with anyone, and that made their inclusion with the firm's affairs a virtual impossibility, especially as the firm was not big enough to carry them financially for the period of time that it would take them to settle in and gain knowledge. At first, there was an impasse, until it was pointed out that the Shopland side wasn't prepared to go along with the idea of an extended family business, and that meant the Mill would close. If that happened, its value would fall dramatically and there would be very little money for anyone, so the sisters withdrew their demand, and Bert had to find the money quickly to pay his sisters out together with the Death Duties.

To raise the necessary cash to achieve this, the old cottage, number 75 in Old Street was sold to build a Fina Petrol Station for Mr Gilbert Thorne, who had a small Garage opposite the Fire Station further down the street. The old forge, shop, and sawmill site in Parnell road were also sold; the Timber stacking ground East of the Sawmills was sold for a new Housing Estate. The Firm was then left with very little ready cash with which to carry on and face the future. Another problem was that David had been commissioned as an Officer while doing his National Service and was thinking about making the Army a career, but changing his mind, he decided to try to buy a Haulage Firm and its Lorries in Newport and so start something new, but delays in settling Edmund's Estate due to family wrangling finally ruled that out.

Eventually, the Estate was settled, and David returned to help his father to run the business. It was decided to try to move out of Clevedon nearer to the new sources of round timber which were mainly the Forestry Commission Forests in South-West England or those in South Wales, so attempts were made to sell the Clevedon site with a view of starting a new Mill near one of those areas, and to that end, sites were visited in the Forest of Dean, the Frome and Taunton Areas, and Devon. But the efforts to sell failed, making moving impossible, so life went more or less back to normal, though times were slowly changing as the war had severely depleted the supply and availability of local standing timber, large Elm Butts to cut boards for the lucrative coffin trade were becoming hard to find, so a second-hand Reciprocating Frame Saw was bought in Nottingham to deal with the Hedgerow tree butts that had been largely ignored before, namely, those that contained the 'farmer's fencing friend'—barbed wire. A chainsaw took the place of the two-man cross-cut handsaw, and the Haigh Bandmill was sold to a firm in Flint.

And yet another problem arose because Bert wanted to take a back seat and leave David to run the Mill, but the staff were upset about that as they were suspicious of a brash ex-Army second Lieutenant taking over and resented the thought of any change. It was also found that buying round timber delivered in was better than purchasing standing timber and renewing the worn-out haulage tackle. Gradually, matters came to a head, ultimatums were issued, and on a sad day, the firm was closed and the men sacked, later, after two weeks, it reopened under David's management, and a new era commenced.

This photo was taken about two weeks after the closure and shows about half of the original workforce.
L-r. Back Row: Harry Hartree. Walt Davis. Ern Scribbins. Charlie Wallis. Eddy Palmer.
Middle row: Reg Youde. George Hartree. Sid Aldom. George Youde. Harold Cole. Frank Gibson.
Seated: Mascot-Stephen Aldom. Mrs Joyce Mills. Herbert Shopland. 'Texas'the Bull Terrier. David Shopland.

In addition, things were rapidly changing worldwide. The British Government was actively encouraging and financing ex-Colonies and undeveloped Countries to build Factories and install British machinery to provide employment and raise standards of living, which meant that the countries supplying the foreign logs started to buy Bandmills and install them near to the forests where the trees grew, so enabling them to export sawn lumber instead of round logs, which was a better use of shipping space as it increased the volume of timber carried and sold. For a while, there was a short increase in second hand wood processing machinery sales, but HM Government never considered the potential long-term loss of jobs and unemployment that would result in England from their foreign 'development' policies or the loss in trade when the new suppliers approached England's customers. But maybe expecting any modern politician to have even a modicum of common or business sense is a futile hope?

By the late 1960s, the large trees had long gone in England, the Foreign log sawmilling trade had greatly diminished, Dutch Elm Disease had removed the Elm Tree forever from the English Countryside, and there was an embargo on all softwood from Wales, owing to an infestation by the Spruce Bark Beetle. The Forestry Commission was starting to release large quantities of softwood on to the market, which was sold in large parcels at regional auctions, and a purchase there required a large cash sum, which at times presented problems. All these changes necessitated a new approach to the Timber trade in England by those still involved in it, which included many wary of any change, such as the Shoplands.

After a great deal of thought, it was decided that the big Stenner Bandmill was no longer needed and should be sold, so a party of African Chiefs escorted by British Colonial Treasury Officials came to Clevedon in a fleet of Rolls-Royce limousines and bought it. The old front gantry was demolished and a new shed built to contain a fully automatic forty-eight-inch Stenner Bandmill complete with loading and unloading gear (log turners, moving table feed, and sawdust extraction plant). Goodyear Tyres rented the original Stenner gantry, and the Sawmills entered into a period of contraction as it had been decided that the way forward was to keep a small nucleus of experienced 'old' hands and recruit new young labour who had no fixed ideas about how things should be run, did what it was told, and didn't argue. David was also heavily involved in managing the local Territorial Army and Cadets in the Drill Hall and was able to provide employment for some of the young recruits. Hardwood supplies had dried up, and softwoods became the mainstay because there was a large market in Clevedon and the surrounding area for carcassing timber for the new housing developments taking place, e.g. Flooring Joists, Roofing materials and flooring. For a while, all seemed well, until the big developers with seemingly limitless money stepped in, outbid local builders for sites, and bought their materials wholesale out of Town.

Fortunately, a share of the timber being produced had been used to supply the pallet trade, and to cope with the extra timber now available from the failed housing contracts, an alliance was made with Rowcliffe Boxes of Bristol for the Sawmills to make pallets for them to sell. Rowcliffes were an old pre-war customer, and the new arrangement worked well for many years. A special pallet-making shed was built, local boys were employed and the world of compressors and nail guns was entered into, and the sawmill was revamped. Elliot Cole returned and became 'engineer in chief' and a good friend to many a young lad having to deal with a new job. Boy management is an art, and Bob Binding took on managing the pallet shop. He had his moments, but overall, things went well, and everyone seemed happy. The Boys were very loyal, and during the winter of 1962/63, when the buses weren't running, several walked from Portishead through five-foot-high snowdrifts every day for a fortnight to come to work. It became cheaper to buy Portuguese pallet-sized timbers than cut them, so the forty-eight-inch Bandmill and thirty-six-inch Band rack were sold to Ransomes of Bishop's Castle and replaced with a forty-two-inch Stenner band rack, a thirty-six-inch Stenner resaw and a Wadkin X-Cut. The gantries had also been replaced by a forklift truck, and that altered the layout of the mill considerably as timber etc. could be placed wherever it was needed. The Office re-entered 71 Old Street using the room where David's Grandmother had done Edmund's accounts on the kitchen Table, and many of the now empty sheds were let to small businesses such as Monsoon Marketing, a clothing wholesale firm, and John Bland, a Builders Merchant. Over the years, the Shopland lorry colours changed from Midland Red to green, then green and red, and finally, to the blue of today. Pallets had to be delivered over a wide area, including five loads of 200 pallets a week to Mardons in Bedminster and 400 per week to Reeds at Newbury. The deliveries had to be reliable and the old lorries had to be scrapped, resulting in Shoplands buying their first brand-new lorry, a Bedford TK, for £1,650 from Welch and Coy of Bristol in 1964. A National Industrial crisis closed the country down, and the resulting two-day week presented problems for a time, but fortunately, the firm was making pallets for food and medical supplies and was allowed to work normally.

Just after the war, Staddons re-emerged and started a small Sawmill in the Old Light Railway Sheds in Lower Queens Road and later moved to the Old Gas-works, where they installed a small Stenner Bandmill. At this time, although the Firm's Sawing capacity had been curtailed, there were Saw Doctor problems through employing part-time people from Bristol, so an arrangement was made to share a Saw Doctor (Charles Bees) with Staddons, which meant that there was a permanent person maintaining the saws of both mills.

At the end of the 1990s, things started to change yet again, and the pallet trade was taken over by two or three large National Firms using fully automated machines to make pallets, which were then hired out to customers for them to use. This was something with which smaller firms were unable to compete, so the Firm started to concentrate on making fence panels until James David's son formed a new company, took over the business in 2018, and returned to selling sawn timber together with fencing panels to the public again.

Maybe caution stopped the Firm from moving too far away from the Hospital as it always provided a backup in case of accidents, and there were quite a few over the years, with several unfortunates being rushed over the road in a wheelbarrow. Fortunately, not many were serious, though one did lead to a Court Case before a Judge in Bristol. In the early days, Edmund's wife was the 'nurse', and any lad feeling poorly was sent to her house in Highdale Avenue, where they would be treated, a case of suspected malingering was rewarded by a large spoonful of Castor Oil and a real sufferer by an aspirin. Minor cuts were painted with Iodine, wasp and bee stings received an application of the blue bag, and any major problems meant the Hospital or the Doctor, but that was a last resort as they both had to be paid for in cash. Dirty necks, knees, hands, and faces were scrubbed with carbolic soap and very long hair, if it were dirty, trimmed with an old pair of sheep shears, which gave the victim a shorn sheepdog look for a little while.

Should this booklet ever be read by decimalised coinage Englishmen, users of dollars and dimes or euros, it might be best to explain a few points, such as in 1914, an English Pound (£1) equalled 4 American Dollars, making one dollar worth 1 Crown or 5 shillings. There were 240 pennies in a Pound, 12 Pennies in a Shilling and 20 shillings in a Pound. 2 ha'pennies in a penny, and 4 farthings in a penny. A half a crown (2/6) was 30 pence. A Florin was 2 shillings. A Golden Sovereign was £1, and a Guinea, £1 and 1 shilling.

Length: 12 inches in a foot, 3 feet in a yard, 1,760 yards in a Statute Mile.

Weight: 14 pounds in a stone, 20 pounds in a score, 112 pounds in a hundredweight, 20 hundredweights in an Imperial ton, and an Imperial ton equals 2,240 lbs.

Signs: A Pound (money) £; a shilling !/-; a penny 1d.

Wages

Wages in a firm are an important item as they form the bond between employer and employee. All labour is done in advance in the trust that the money earned will be paid when it is due, normally at the end of the week or month. Shoplands are proud to say that they have always paid on time. Wages are also a good indicator of the health of the working relationships within a firm, for if the names do not change too often, it means that the majority of the employees are happy and satisfied. Looking back, it would seem that this was the case with the Mill as many, when they left, had worked there for over forty years, some a lifetime, and others left and returned several times.

When William started in business, wages were minimal, and most poor people lived on the edge of subsistence levels. Small businessmen were at times marginally a little better off than the people they employed as most had to borrow money to finance their enterprises and so were often struggling to make ends meet. What was paid by Shoplands in those very early days are now not known as there are no Wage Books left from before 1900, probably because when William's two eldest sons settled up his Estate, they were considered to be of little interest or value. However, I suspect that a labourer's wage at that time was in the region of twelve to fourteen shillings per week, with a Craftsman being paid a few more shillings. The six-day week had no set hours and was from early Monday morning until Saturday Teatime; you started very early in the morning and worked until the job was done, and sometimes that included nights. There is a record on a slip of paper that says that in 1898, the Traction Engine had to earn £5 per week to show a small profit after paying wages for three men, running costs, and loan repayment monies.

In 1897, when Edmund started trading on his own, wages were still much as they were in his Father's day, with a skilled labourer earning

16/- per week if he were lucky. Later, when workmen were paid by the hour and a working week included Saturday, the working day started at 6 a.m.; breakfast, 7 a.m. to 8 a.m.; work, 8 a.m. to 1 p.m.; dinner, 1 p.m. to 2 p.m.; then work again from 2 p.m. to 6 p.m. or until the job was finished, with Saturday finishing at 4 p.m., totalling fifty-three working hours plus per week. Conditions improved in the late 1930s and, together with improved mechanisation, meant that Saturday afternoons were not worked and a later daily start at 8 a.m. made a forty-eight-hour week, which lasted until the early 1950s. Tea breaks were unknown and didn't come into being until in wartime Britain during 1940; a tea ration to supplement a manual workers meagre food ration was issued.

On the whole, over the years, matters regarding pay within the Firm were decided amicably, except on one occasion when the boys making boxes staged Clevedon's first labour strike, when after their demand on a fine, sunny summer Monday morning for more money was refused, they withdrew their labour and went off to play football on Salthouse Fields. It was only solved at the end of the first week when their irate mothers came to the Office to see why their sons had not been paid for their week's work. When they were told what had happened, Mother 'power' soon restored order, and a very chastened junior workforce came in on Monday to ask for their jobs back. Edmund was inclined at first to say No and give the boys the sack, but he relented when his Wife reminded him that he had been young once. The Strike was nearly as important an event to the Town as its first mechanical road Vehicle accident in 1903 when Shopland's new Traction Engine finished up completely in the ditch opposite Marshal's cottage in Moor Lane (Later Holland's Pottery).

I suspect that My Father was the most understanding employer to date in the Family as he would listen, sympathise, and endeavour to reach an agreement, whereas his Father and Grandfather worked more or less on the principle of 'If I pay, I say and it goes my way!' as did his son. But we have always accepted the principle of 'A fair day's work is worth a fair day's pay' and listened to reasoned argument, even when times have been hard.

It must be pointed out that to endeavour to draw any comparisons as to then and now is very difficult and almost a waste of time as circumstances have greatly changed over the years, because what our forebears expected to do and be able to buy with their money is very different to what is expected as the norm today, so the only way to gain some indication is by comparing the work time needed to purchase a single item or finance a simple task, as an illustration, I will use a conversation I had recently with a young Barber who was earning around £320 a week. Haircuts are now mostly £10, so he has to achieve thirty-two haircuts each week to cover his pay. In 1939, wages were £1.50 to £2 per week, so at 240 old pennies to the pound and haircuts costing 3 pence for a man and half of that for a child, he would have had to ensure at least two hundred heads to make up his wages, and it must be remembered that they had to finance any sick pay and their retirement monies themselves out of their weekly wage with no help from the State or their Employer.

The following pages have been extracted from old wage books and are included to show how wages and costs have increased over the years.

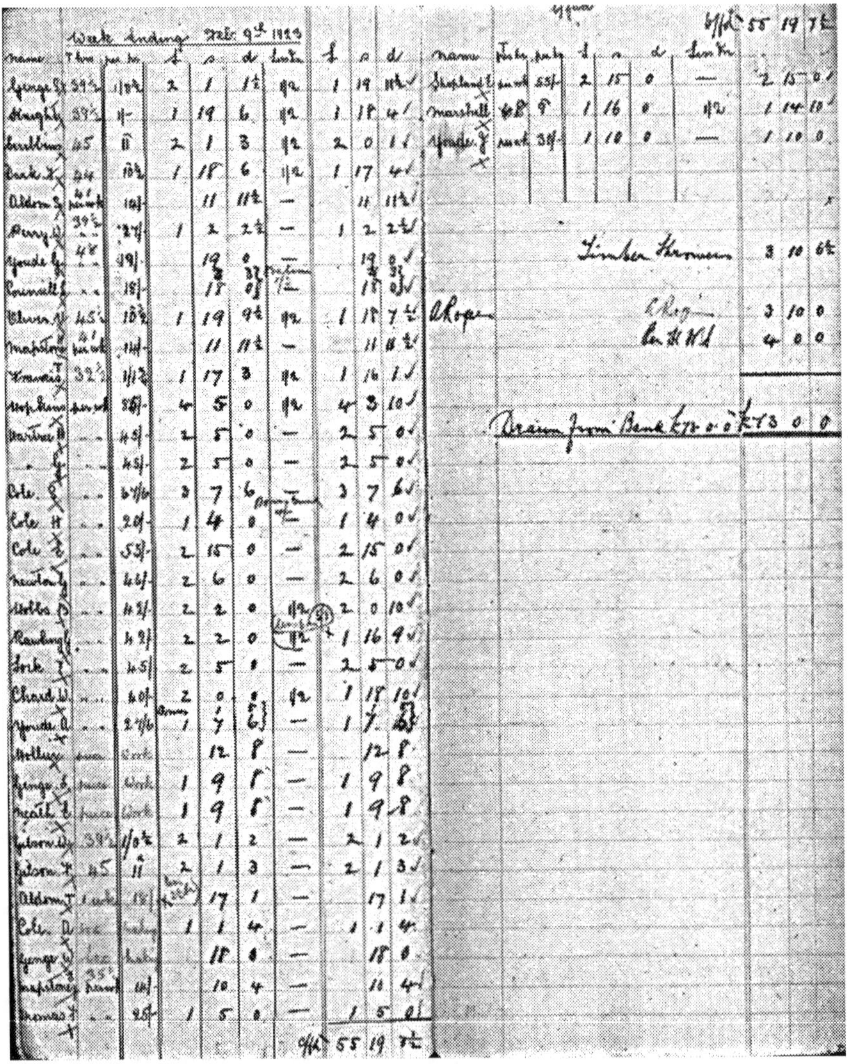

Wages 1923

Wages 1933

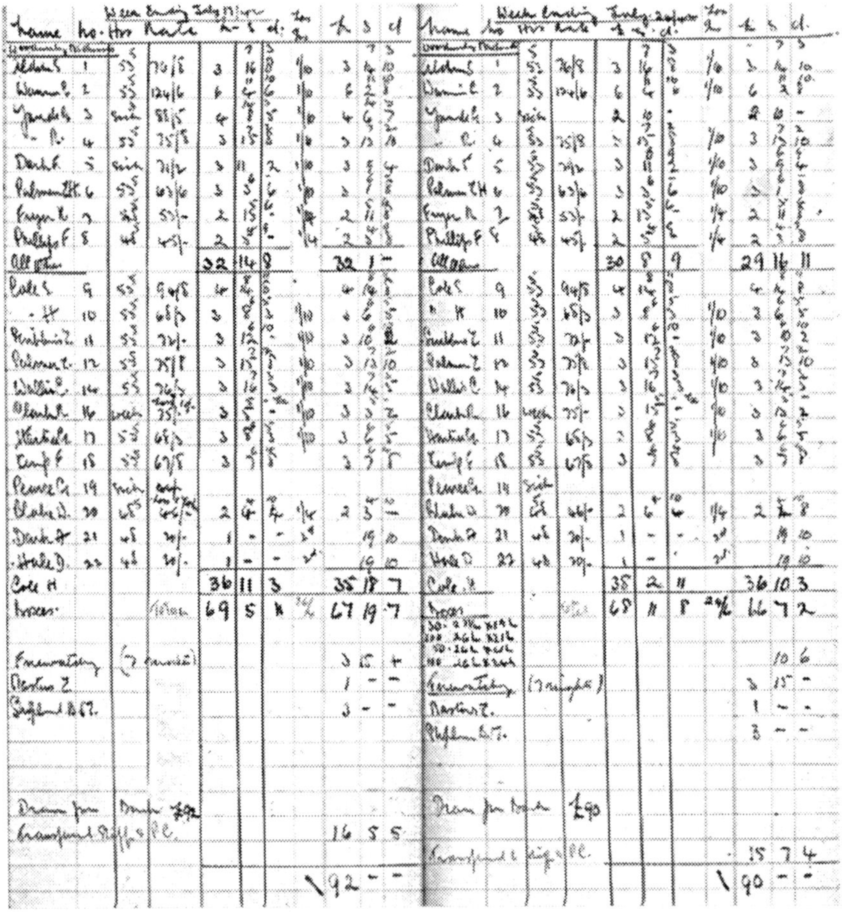

Name No. Hrs Rate £ s d £ s d

Week Ending July

32 14 8 32 1 –

36 11 3 35 18 7

69 5 11 67 19 7

3 15 4

1 – –

3 – –

16 5 5

£92 – –

30 8 9 29 16 11

38 2 11 36 10 3

68 11 8 66 7 2

10 6

3 15 –

1 – –

3 – –

15 7 4

£90 – –

Wages 1942

Rate	M/c	Name		Gross Pay	Insurance	Less Insurance	Income Tax	Wage Paid
		Woodworking &c						
1	112/11	45	Aldous. J.	41	5 12 11	4 11	5 8 ·	3 ·	5 5 ·
3	125/11	45	Yandle L.G	89	6 5 11	4 11	6 1 ·	—	6 1 ·
1	113/11	46	Yandle R.J.	90	5 13 5	4 11	5 10 6	—	5 10 6
5	113/11	45	Pearce H.G.	41	5 12 11	4 11	5 8 ·	2 ·	5 6 ·
7	100/-	45	Rowland R.G	34	5 · ·	4 11	4 15 1	7 ·	4 8 1
			All others		28 7 2		12 72 7		26 10 4
2	151/11	45	Ralph J	90	7 17 11	4 11	7 13 ·	5 ·	7 8 ·
9	128/10	40	Cole N.C	29	5 14 6	4	5 14 2	13 ·	5 1 2
8	108/11	45	Cole P.H	86	5 8 11	4 11	5 4 ·	—	5 4 ·
11	114/11	45	Sanders E.H.	36	5 14 11	4 11	5 10 ·	10 ·	5 · ·
12	105/11	45	Palmer E.	105	5 5 11	4 11	5 1 ·	—	5 1 ·
14	79/4	28	Wallis. C.	60	3 3 6	4 11	2 18 7	—	2 18 7
6	101/11	45	Hartnell L.E.	36	5 1 11	4 11	4 17 ·	7 ·	4 10 ·
17	112/11	45	Watson C.	89	5 12 11	4 11	5 8 ·	—	5 8 ·
19	107/11	45	Badman N.A.	34	5 7 11	4 11	5 3 ·	8 ·	4 15 ·
21	90/-	45	Hartnell J.H	28	4 10 ·	4	4 9 8	6 ·	4 3 8
22	56/-	45	Badman R	34	2 6 ·	2 10	2 7 2	—	2 7 2
23	102/11	45	Mann L.J	64	5 2 11	4 11	4 18 ·	1 ·	4 17 ·
24	50/-	45	Shopland R.W.	·	2 10 ·	2 10	2 7 2	—	2 7 2
			Office		64 1 4		161 10 9		59 · 9
26	130/-	43	Pendar D.W.	34	6 10 ·	4 11	6 5 1	13 ·	5 12 1
					70 11 4		167 15 10		64 12 10
					98 18 6	4 · 1	144 18 5	3 15 ·	41 3 5

Wages 1948

I have not included details of wages since 1948 as with people still alive who drew them matters could become a little contentious. But after the war, Wage tribunals were established for most trades, and they ensured that there were National Wage structures that kept abreast of inflation etc. and removed much of the need for local individual negotiation.

People involved in the Office

1896–1918: Lizzie Shopland (Edmund's wife)
1918–1939: Mr Rogers
1920–1926: Dora Shopland
1939–1946: Byrde Shopland, Kathleen Shopland (Bert's Wife)
1946–1951: Derek Pendar

1951–1957: Mrs Flo Hack
1957–1965: Mrs Joyce Mills
1965–1971: D. W. Shopland
1971–2018: Ann Shopland (David's wife)

TRANSPORT

Horses: Nib carriage, wooden four-wheeled timber carriage, and carts
Steam: Traction Engines, Locomotives (Burrell and Foster)
Steam Waggons: Sentinel and Foden
Petrol: Lorries and Tractors

Lorries

Pre-1930: AEC, Albion, Dennis, Guy
1930–1946: Bristol, Dennis, Commer, Guy,
Leyland, Morris Commercial, Fordson
1947–2018: Crossley, AEC, Dodge, Bedford, Nissan

Cars

1910–2018: KRIT, Minerva, Sunbeam, Singer, Ford, Bean,
Morris Cowley, Wolseley, Vauxhall, Armstrong-Siddeley,
Sunbeam-Talbot, Rover, Austin, Riley, Hillman, BMW

Burrell at Flax Bourton. Believe Driver to
be Tom Sparkes, rest unknown.
Only first waggon lettered with Edmund's name. c.1903

Sentinel Steam Waggon Hauling Bricks to build
Wake And Deans Furniture Factory at Yatton.
Taken near to Portbury House on Yatton Road.
(Hangstone Houses above Quarry in background.)
L-r : Sam Cole (Driver).Herbert Shopland (Boy Mate), c 1912.

<u>Illustration of Fordson Industrial Tractor used for Timber
Haulage. Shopland's model had no cab. c .1935.</u>
<u>Typical between the Wars Transport</u>

When the War was over, there was a great and urgent need to replace most of the civilian vehicles that had been used during the war as many were pre-war and worn out. Spares were virtually unobtainable as the number of vehicles produced before the War had been relatively few and models and designs had changed almost yearly. For nearly ten years post-1945, all new commercial vehicles and cars went for export to earn foreign cash to buy raw materials and food, the only exceptions being those required for Military and Emergency Services or specialist civilian use, e.g. Doctors, Civil Servants, Tax Inspectors. But to compensate for this, there were vast numbers of ex-Military vehicles being sold countrywide by auction without a monetary reserve, so Shoplands packed some cash and went forth to hopefully buy.

It was the first time that four-wheel-drive vehicles were on sale in any quantity, many of which were ideal for timber haulage and extraction. American vehicles such as the Diamond T, Mack, or the Ward de la France were left-hand drive and, in the main, too large and cumbersome for Somerset lanes and byways; Quads were too small, larger Bedfords, Morrises, Austins, and Fords were not structurally substantial enough, though a QL was bought to serve as a Yard lorry. Scammell and Albion Gun Tractors were too slow and heavy, and that left only the Crossley for Shoplands to purchase, as the AEC Matador was Diesel-powered and therefore an unknown quantity. Crossley Airfield Fire tenders were the first to be bought, as although they had a power take-off to which a winch could be fitted, they were of little use to the average business outside of the Timber Trade.

As trade expanded, more vehicles were put on the road, and at their height, there were three tractors and Timber carriages, a Crossley artic, and two yard lorries. But this only lasted for about ten years as trade changed, with more round timber being bought and delivered in, which resulted in less self-haulage and less haulage vehicles. Several experiments were made to put diesel engines into Crossley chassis, but only Gardiner engines were readily available, and they were too big. Perkins Diesels came shortly afterwards but were temperamental about starting in cold weather and, being new, were expensive. Automower was an engineering firm at Norton St Phillips near Bath, and they, amongst other things, specialised in making and adapting vehicle and machinery for the Home-Grown Timber Trade. Mr Grice, their Managing Director, was a personal friend of Edmund, and they exchanged ideas and supplied the firm with many items, as did Bird's Engineering in Albert Road in Bristol who made the special metal bits and pieces that Edmund couldn't make in the forge.

Eddy Palmer (Driver) and Bedford QL 1949 after
conversion for civilian use. c, 1948.
Roof of second wooden Yard Office across river behind lorry.

Typical Crossley Lorry as bought at Army Vehicle Auction

Crossley Artic with William's Three Sons and Bert
L – R. Edmund, John and Charles c. 1947

Morris Quad similar to Guy that was briefly used in yard.

The seven-ton Dodge 'Kew' in the background was one of the most difficult vehicles to buy as it was one of twenty identical lorries on offer in Bristol, and where do you start to choose? The Austin nearest was a converted two-ton van from Gibbs, the wholesale chemists in Bristol, and was driven by Peter Davies. The sack trucks in the foreground were one of the oldest forms of transport ever owned by the firm and still exist.

Timber Felling and Hauling

Timber throwers were often made up of family Groups, and in this part of North Somerset, the Dingleys of West End, Nailsea, were recognised as being second to none, and it is reputed that they were of Romany origin. All 'throwers' took great pride in their tools and maintained them to a high standard as their livings and that of their families depended on them. Blunt axes or saws meant harder work and more time spent on a particular job. All tools were oiled and kept well wrapped when not in use, and woe betide anyone who 'borrowed' one of them without asking.

Throwing Timber was a very skilled trade and very hard work. While Shoplands had a few 'fellers' on the Staff for small and special one-off jobs, the larger parcels of timber were mostly contracted out to self employed Timber Fellers who travelled ahead of the hauliers and when the felled tree was on the ground with its branches removed were paid by the cubic foot. It was not always possible to check their figures on a daily basis, so they were given their money on an estimated weekly basis, which, in the final analysis, meant that the tally of felled timber had to relate to the amount of the volume estimated to have been in the trees when they were standing, and that made purchasing a very skilled art. In later years, the 'fellers' travelled with the Tractor which removed what they had cut down that day.

Harry Scribbins's 1928 Timber Throwers Record Book
<u>Paid roughly 1.5d per cubic foot.</u>

(Note the old practice of signing over two
penny stamps when issuing receipt.)
<u>Harry Scribbins was a long time employee of the Firm and gave
invaluable assistance to my Father in his Farming enterprises.)</u>

Hand Felling large tree with x cut saw, ropes attached to handles allow two extra men to help pull the saw through the cut.

Although using the chainsaw for felling became a universal common practice, Shoplands always had reservations and used a handsaw if they were felling a specimen or special tree, as taking longer to cut the tree through gave more control over the felling process and enabled preventative measures to be taken in time, if for instance there were a danger of the tree splitting or falling in the wrong direction, though that was a rare occurrence as the fellers prided themselves on being able to place a fallen tree on a line drawn from it in the dirt. But few of these skills were needed when in 1988, many trees were blown down in the great Gale that swept through England. Hauliers from all over the Country were involved in clearing the fallen trees and delivering them to Sawmills, and the Clevedon Sawmills took in timber from as far afield as North Yorkshire and the Home Counties.

Demise of Edward V11's Coronation Elm at
Newhouse Farm Clevedon (Moor Lane)
L-r. L Mann. E Scribbins. K Brimble. C. 1949.
Note - No Jib on Matador, seat for extra crew
(Timber Throwers) to ride behind cab.

Sadly, the Coronation tree stood in a small triangle of open ground surrounded by made-up roads, and over the years, the constant passing traffic had adversely affected its roots, causing it to die and have to be felled. It is believed that it's commemorative plaque now resides in the little museum contained in the former farmyard.

Tree Felling and Cross cutting Machinery

ELLING WITH THE WITTE SAW

purchasing the Witte Saw, w. Tree Felling Contractor, v a lifetime felling trees by was not an advocate of v. HE IS NOW !

Thousands in Use.

We can't print the names of o x purchasers of WITTE POWER SAWS, but here are some :

THE WAR OFFICE
THE COLONIAL OFFICE
GUEST, KEEN & NETTLEFOLDS, LTD.
GREGOR BROS. LTD., SWANSEA
J. B. KEMP & SONS, LTD., ROSS
ELECTRIC SAWMILLS, BRIGHTON
CAHIR SAWMILLS, TIPPERARY
CROWN SAWMILLS, KEIGHLEY
WILLOWDALE SAWMILLS, ABERDEEN
BALTIC SAWMILLS, AMMANFORD
TOLPUTT'S STEAM SAWMILLS, DOVER
SALOP TIMBER CO., SHREWSBURY
J. & S. AGATE, LTD., HORSHAM
WENBAN-SMITH, LTD., WORTHING
SHUTEND SAWMILLS, DUDLEY
WATERFALL SAWMILLS, OLDHILL
GEO. RANDALL & SON, LTD., BRIDGWATER
MONMOUTH STEAM SAWMILLS
ROBERTS & HIRST, LTD., HALIFAX
HORROX & CO., LTD., SHEFFIELD
W. L. EDGOOSE SAWMILLS, GODALMING
RUDDERS & PAYNES, LTD., BIRMINGHAM
JOHN KELLY, LTD., BELFAST
T. A. EVERTON, DROITWICH
A. TURNER & SON, LTD., LEWES
DARBY BROS. LTD., BECCLES
W. S. WELLS, HUNTINGDON
J. QUALTROUGH & CO., CASTLETOWN, I.O.M.
G. HALSEY & SONS, ENFIELD
W. WRIGHT & SONS, LTD., CHESHAM
JAS. CONSTANCE & SONS, LONGHOPE
T. S. SHILL, CHELTENHAM

THE WITTE PORTABLE POWER SAW

The Timber Merchant's "Handy-Man."

SPLITTING MAHOGANY LOGS for Messrs. Gillies & Co., Importers, Liverpool.

"The WITTE Saw is splitting big logs 20ft. long with remarkable accuracy. This we may tell you we consider to be a wonderful thing."
A. H. GILLIES.

CANADIAN IMPORTERS, LTD
AVONMOUTH, BRISTOL

CLARIDGE & CO., LTD.

Heythrop Sawmills
CHIPPING NORTON

The WITTE Saw is never idle very long in Messrs. Claridge's Yard at Heythrop, where they do not believe in using skilled labour on work that a machine will do in a quarter the time and at a fraction of the cost.

FOREST PRODUCTS, LTD.

HUNTLEY, Glos.

After eight years use without an overhaul, Mr. Bayliss, the manager, says of the WITTE Saw:

"It is a marvellous little machine, always ready for work, never any trouble, which is all the more remarkable, seeing that it has always been handled by unskilled labour."

F. J. GILLAM,

Ashley Down Sawmills
BRISTOL

Mounted on pneumatic road-wheels because it is being constantly moved from one yard to another, the WITTE Saw tackles all sorts and sizes of timber. "I could not be without the Witte Saw," says Mr. Gillam. "It is invaluable."

As will be seen, there was a great demand locally for these saws, but unfortunately, although Shoplands were one of the first Firms to buy one, it could be that their possibly making a late payment excluded them from the sales brochure.

Long loads

Sometimes there was a call for special long timbers or steel girders, and they could be over one hundred feet in length. The maximum that Shoplands were ever asked to cut was one special beam forty feet in length, which caused many problems and prompted the decision never to do anything like it again regardless of what the customer might pay. Trees to cut such timbers could be hauled in the length required, and this caused many problems with other traffic on the pre-Motorway roads, but as they were classed as 'indivisible' loads, they were allowed on the highway. Herbert was a Councillor on the Clevedon Urban District Council, and a scheme was put forward to make part of the Triangle one way for traffic. This was to divert the traffic from Kenn Road into Station Road and then into Old Church Road. Herbert objected and said that large lorries would not be able to negotiate such a system and was told that such a statement was ridiculous, so being challenged, he said that if the Committee would pay for any damage, he would prove that his statement was true. The Committee accepted the challenge, and Shopland's Tractor and Timber carriage carrying several trees fifty feet in length started to attempt to travel round the proposed route. Halfway round, Herbert had to stop the demonstration as the vehicle and load would have removed the wall holding up the top storey of the Bristol Cooperative Society's Grocery store, which was at the end of Station Road where it joined Old Church Road, with disasterous results for the Coop. The Committee, realising that to complete the demonstration would cost them a lot of money, agreed to quietly drop the scheme and to leave matters as they were.

AEC – artic, typical of vehicle delivering to Yard. Load is a 'Solitary parkland oak, note size of tree and how rough it is.

Traction Engine Timber Hauling in Nightingale Valley Weston in Gordano. L-R: G Youde. G Rawlings. S Coles. c 1920.

Crossley Artic carrying Sweet Chestnut at Brockley c, 1949
L-R - D Badman. C Watson EHS. E Scribbins.

Timber felling and Hauling was another way of life, up and about early in the morning and home late at night. Meals were taken on the job and were often just a sandwich, lump of cheese and bread, or just an apple, all washed down with some water, cold tea from a bottle, or if you were very lucky, a cup of hot tea brought out by the Farmer's wife. You were wet when it rained, dry when the sun shone, and sometimes just cold, but you were always dirty. However, to a degree, you were your own boss, worked at your own pace, fixed the amount of your wages if you were on piecework and you could always leave and find another job if you were fed up. Your tools were yours, and you kept and maintained them, for their sharpness made the work easy or hard. Occasionally, the job was far away from home, and you slept where you could, and if you were lucky like George, you could find a warm and dry manger filled with warm hay in a cowshed where you could spend a comfortable night, though explaining it to the large, puzzled, and somewhat agitated Bull wanting his breakfast in the morning was a little difficult and could necessitate a very quick strategic withdrawal. Washing and Toilets were never mentioned, for it was a simple and hard life.

Crossley Artic in Yard.

EHS. Viewing Tyntesfield Elm on Home-made carriage
before being rolled off onto ground as it was too heavy
for the 5 ton Gantry crane to handle, C.1948.

Bedford QL Artic in rough conditions on the Cotswold Hills

Although the stated purpose of the Sawmills was to deal in wood, there were sometimes odd jobs that arose because someone was in trouble, happened to be a friend, or no one else would do it, such as raising lintels and putting them in place on a local new church. Helping a farmer with his haymaking so as not to spoil the crop with felled trees, pulling the odd horse or cow out from where it was stuck in a ditch. Rescuing a Clevedon Territorial Army Truck from Weston sands on a Sunday morning before the incoming tide engulfed it, and later the same week, saving a broken-down digger from the Marine Lake in Clevedon before it suffered a similar fate. Also, providing extra hands to carry large patients upstairs in the local Hospital, helping the undertaker's bearers to lift a heavy coffin out of an upstairs window, making floats on lorries for the carnival procession, transport for Sunday school outings, helping to erect large Christmas trees, supplying the timber and building platforms for Choral Society recitals in various local Halls, working a snow plough to keep the roads free in the bad winter of 1963, and many other things, including supplying the odd bit of wood to all and sundry when it was needed, all mostly for nothing as that was part of the privilege of being part of a community living in a small Town.

Matador crane Installing Petrol Tanks at Kenn Garage
for Mr Holtham c. 1960 DWS positioning Tank.

In distance houses in Parnell Rd. before
construction of Teignmounth Rd.
Yard looking from Drying Shed through Gantry to Parnell
Rd before the construction of Teignmouth Rd.
The shed with the white door seen through Gantry is
Mr Blackmore's Garage by Roger's Barbers shop and left
of road to back of Sawmills i.e. New St. c. 1945.

Looking across Old Light Railway track from
allotments toward new Gantry and shed c.1945.
Remains of light Railway Track fence in fore-ground.

Later view of Back of Sawmills showing new dropped kerb
from Teignmouth Rd and disused wooden Gate from old
rear entrance through New St. from Parnal Road.

Over the years, the Sawmills has provided an income and a livelihood for many people and overall made a profit, but success comes at a price, and maybe it was the Shopland Wives who paid most of it, for it was they who managed on very little housekeeping money, whose new furniture was a new machine or vehicle for the yard, who scrimped and saved to find a little money for a spare part in times of dire need, who never complained, had no real holidays, listened to all of the grumbling, and who went without. Margaret, Lizzie, Kathleen, and Ann all paid a high price to support their Husbands' endeavours and were not always given the credit that was due to them.

Although at times it was hard going, it was not always doom and gloom, and there were lighter moments, such as when an employee chopping firewood, chopped off one of his wooden legs by mistake and had to be taken home in a wheelbarrow. When he returned after dinner, it was realised that if the other leg were made shorter, he would be able to walk again, so he went home for tea much reduced in stature. The Steam waggon driver who crashed into a pond and then rang the office to ask where he could obtain water to fill up the engine's boiler; the reply was best forgotten. The fire-watching piquet who ran past the new cabinet of fire extinguishers with buckets of water from the river to fight a fire. A bright young spark who, being unable to remove some large tyres from their wheels, put them into the base of the yard Boiler chimney, set fire to them, and disappeared from sight in the smokescreen that enveloped the lower Town.

However that was all long ago and it took a more recent generation to liven things up again. It was Derek clad only in a cotton singlet and underpants who was found by the police riding his bike over Salisbury Plain in the deep snow and the ice of the coldest winter experienced since the Middle Ages and his only explanation was that he was late for work and must have taken the wrong turning, the brother chasing his sibling around the Mill with an axe intent on doing harm because the latter had eaten his sandwiches and the tale of another pair, one of whom was hidden in the Boss's front room on a Sunday afternoon, until his brother, who was hunting for him, could be persuaded to give up a carving knife and return home. There was also the case of the qualified Territorial Army Driver who failed to check the water in his truck and blew the engine up when delivering timber to Bristol. But as Herbert would have said that was part of the rich tapestry of life and should be treated as such.

And things did not always go according to plan, for there was the major problem caused when the mason building the new Boiler Chimney refused to go higher than thirty feet as he thought that the ground was a long way down from where he was working, and it was only after he was taken up the scaffolding, the ladders removed, leaving him marooned in space for three days and two nights which enabled him to make sure that the structure was finished at the required forty feet. The old lady who was afraid to leave her bungalow in case it should be damaged by a large Elm tree that was being felled in her neighbour's garden; after a long debate, she was persuaded to go shopping in Bristol, which was fortunate, as the tree was hollow and fell the wrong way, causing a large branch to go through her bungalow roof. Hurried repairs by a local builder put things right before the old dear returned, and all was well, though she often wondered why she later found some green elm leaves under her bed. Sadly, everyone had fled, leaving no one prepared to tell how they had got there. A time when a wheel came off a loaded timber carriage when it was descending a steep hill and overtook the tractor, finishing up leaning against the Public bar of a pub at the bottom of the hill where it had to stay until the local Bobby (Policeman) had been persuaded to forget that anything untoward might have happened by being entertained in the Pub's other bar. A large 'monkey puzzle' tree at Langford which jumped to the left after it was cut completely through at the base and remained leaning on the glass roof of a large conservatory without breaking a pane of glass. There are more tales that could be told, but perhaps if they were, it might foster the erroneous belief that Shoplands did not always employ the wisest and brightest in the Town or because they weren't brainy enough to do so.

The Sawmills have changed greatly over the years, and there is little left of the original buildings. Edmund's forge still exists and is capable of being used should another 'Vulcan' appear, and the Boiler house and chimney still stand as a testament to past endeavours. I have threatened to place a statue of Puck with his hand to his nose, making a rude gesture, on the chimney's top. It would revolve in the wind and show to everyone the family's opinion of Authority in all its forms. But it is doubtful if it will ever happen for in the words of a very old music hall song, 'My wife won't let me!'.

There is little left to say, and this has been written 270 years after my relation was in business dealing with wood in Devon. How much further back written records exist for the Family is not known. It is 170 years since the Shoplands came to Clevedon, and I do not know if there will be anyone from the family able to add to this tale in a hundred years' time, but if there is, I hope that they will be as awkward and single-minded as we were, enjoy the same amount of goodwill as we have, and that they experience as much fun in life as as we have.

Whether as a Family we have contributed greatly to the Town's prosperity, improved its standing in Society, raised or maintained its morals, or done any lasting good is problematical and not for me to say. BUT! We have had a wonderful time, earned a shilling, made friends, and done our best, and Clevedon has been good to us. Looking back the firm had many loyal and conscientious employees who could always be relied upon and did their best whatever the circumstances and without such helpers the firm would never have survived or lasted so long. And after eighty years of continuous involvement with the Sawmills I find it humbling that I can still go to any of the employees past or present, have a friendly word or seek advise or help. Any of which will be freely given. Maybe that in the end is possibly what life and business should be about?

As for the future, well, it is before us, and time inevitably marches on, so as we advance into the unknown, we would do well to remember the pop star Alma Coghlan, who sang a famous song, 'Que sera, sera' (Whatever will be, will be), and no doubt that will prove to be true. Hopefully, there will still be some trees to fell, and Shoplands' Sawmills will still be around somewhere in Clevedon in a hundred years' time. But whether there will be any large quantity of timber to sell will be problematic, as now World supplies and reserves are diminishing, and Lloyd George's Forestry Commission in England has ceased to plant trees to create a Timber reserve in Times of need. Where will Timber, the ever-adaptable raw material, come from? As the present Forestry policy is to plant mainly trees for Biomass fuels and wood pulp for paper, which are harvested after thirty years of growth. A sizeable tree for timber takes at least one hundred and twenty to fifty years to mature!

However going back to our possible Roman roots 'nil desperandum', for in the words of the Weston Grammar School Motto the only way for the Family to go if it is to survive in the coming modern age is by going: 'EVER FORWARD' and now that Ann and I have retired I have no doubt that James and his new team will work hard to enable the new Company, Shoplands The Clevedon Sawmills Ltd. to have a bright and prosperous Future.

A tailpiece giving Food for thought?

Throughout this tale, the Family has always had many assets but never large amounts of ready cash, and that fact has overshadowed many decisions, and maybe Herbert's theory that a modest overdraft at the Bank is a good thing may still be true, as it can always curtail reckless and spontaneous spending.

APPENDIX

For many readers, the names of the machines that are used for cutting trees into usable timber mean very little, so the following are some illustrations of those in common usage. They are of the 1920s era and, although dated, are typical indicators as to the similar types of machinery to be found in modern Sawmills. Other than the Haigh Bandmill my Grandfather preferred to deal with, local manufacturers such as Stenners of Tiverton and Eastman and Johnson of Taunton, as their spares and advice, were nearer at hand if needed.

<u>Log Conversion Machinery</u>

The first real mechanical improvement with log sawing after the Pit Saw came with the invention of the reciprocating log saw commonly known as the Horizontal Frame Saw, which had a saw blade on a sliding frame which moved rapidly from left to right as the log was drawn through it on a moving carriage. Some of its successors cut vertically and had multiple blades in a frame which produced several boards at each cut. Such machines made the 'primary' cut in the conversion of a tree into sawn planks and therefore had to be large and robustly constructed. The saw blades were hand-sharpened, and by today's standards, it was a very slow machine, only cutting at a rate of less than two feet per minute, producing boards and flitches up to ten inches in thickness.

Horizontal Frame saw

The next major development in log conversion was the Horizontal Bandmill using a Bandsaw instead of blade. The very large machines had wheels up to 108 inches in diameter and were able to cut deep sections of timber over 40 inches in thickness far quicker than the preceding reciprocating machine. The main drawback to both machines being that it was necessary to have some lifting aid nearby to place a log on the machine and remove heavy planks after they had been cut. The saw also had to be raised when returning the tree for the next cut and then reset.

Horizontal Bandmill

The Vertical Bandmill soon overtook the Horizontal in popularity as it was a faster cutting machine for smaller thicknesses as the logs could be loaded from a stage without the need of a crane, and the sawn boards easily fell away without any manual assistance on to a moving conveyor belt, which quickly removed them. The boards produced were mainly 'through and through', having wane on both sides i.e. bark. In America, where the trees were larger, the wheel size could be as large as 120 inches (10 feet) or over, with the Bandsaw blade being thicker with teeth on both sides to enable the tree to be cut continuously as the carriage move backwards and forwards.

Vertical Bandmill and carriage

Following a Bandmill, there had to be a machine that would saw the timber produced by them into smaller sizes when required and also deal with the small round logs. This was the job of the Band Rack, which was a very good machine, though it could largely only produce planks or boards having one square edge. Early rack benches used a circular saw with a wooden table, with many being portable and driven by power supplied from a belt driven from the flywheel of a stationary Traction engine or a waterwheel, later models used a band Saw and were electrically powered.

Band rack saw

The final machines in the breaking-down process were the circular saws which dealt with the more easily handled smaller timbers and, in many cases, turned the offcuts into firewood.

Circular Sawbench

There are many other smaller machines used in Sawmills, such X-cuts, Planers, etc., but their use is common and known to many other trades, so they are not included here.

DAVID W. SHOPLAND

SYNOPSIS

This is a story of a Family who were typical of their time and class, namely, people who had and expected very little but soldiered on and did the tasks that they were set, grumbled all the way, and had lots of fun, whilst establishing a business in a developing small Town during one of England's most exciting and turbulent times, when international conflict and social reform dominated lives.

It is a record of endeavour, minor persecution, together with the history of a typical small lower middle-class family who struggled to survive and finally succeeded against opposition and adversity. A story about people and human nature, persons who believed in Divine Providence and by serving others, were humbled and exalted in equal measure.

BIOGRAPHY

David Shopland has been happily married to his wife, Ann, for fifty years, is a Family man with two children and four grandchildren. He was born in Clevedon, Somerset into a happy and loving home during the 1930s Depression. Brought up in a farming environment, he now runs a Family business of Timber Merchants and Sawmill Owners dating back into the early 1700s. A teenager during the War, he was Educated at a State Grammar School and completed twenty-five years Commissioned Service as an Officer in The Royal Artillery, Territorial Army, and Army Cadet Force. He has enjoyed being a Local Authority Councillor for nearly forty years and has just finished being Chairman of both a Town and Unitary Authority Council. He is a Military Vehicle and Vintage Car enthusiast, small Livestock Breeder and Exhibitor, and Founder of a successful Youth Club, a Fighter of apparent lost causes and was recently described in the local Press as being his Town's equivalent of 'Prince Phillip Duke of Edinburgh'. He believes in a Divine Providence and, having survived a second childhood, is sure, in his own mind that he is now a second-generation teenager with all that it implies.

The Sawmills, Old Street, Clevedon, Somerset, BS21 6BT, GB.
Tel.: 01275-874121

Printed in the United States
by Baker & Taylor Publisher Services